FIRE IN THE BLOOD

Gennie Durham buys into the Flying Fox country pub, and finds herself in the middle of a Yorkshire murder mystery — with Oliver Hammond, the man she is becoming increasingly attracted to, as the prime suspect. But there's worse to come . . . An arsonist is on the loose in Fenwick-cum-Marton. The historic St Stephen's Church has already been burned to the ground. Is Gennie's pub next on the fire-raiser's list?

RENA GEORGE

FIRE IN THE BLOOD

Complete and Unabridged

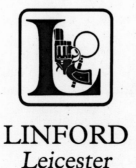

LINFORD
Leicester

First published in Great Britain in 2013

First Linford Edition
published 2014

A catalogue record for this book is available
from the British Library.

ISBN 978–1–4448–2160–4

Published by
F. A. Thorpe (Publishing)
Anstey, Leicestershire

Set by Words & Graphics Ltd.
Anstey, Leicestershire
Printed and bound in Great Britain by
T. J. International Ltd., Padstow, Cornwall

This book is printed on acid-free paper

1

'But you can't do that!' Gennie Durham was on her feet, fist thumping the table. 'You can't sell the Flying Fox. I won't let you!'

Mitch Hammond looked away and cleared his throat. His wife Molly's eyes rounded with surprise at the outburst.

'She's right, Dad.' Oliver Hammond was on his feet. 'Gennie's a shareholder in the company just like the rest of us. She's entitled to have her say.' He shot a glance to his brother, expecting Will's support, but the younger man just shrugged, his disinterested frown sliding from one to the other.

Gennie's eyebrow arched. Oliver had never gone out of his way to support her before. Now that she thought about it, she couldn't remember him ever showing any real interest in the family pub business either. He was a successful architect with a suite of riverside offices in York. So why was he suddenly jumping to her defence?

Molly put up her hands in a gesture that said, stay calm. 'Of course you're all entitled to have your say,' she reasoned. 'That's why we've called this meeting. Your father was just putting forward the options.'

The Hammonds had been running the village pub in Fenwick-cum-Marton for as long as anyone could remember. Before Mitch and Molly, it had been Mitch's father, Dan, who ran the hostelry. A Flying Fox had stood on this site for centuries, and had always thrived.

Will and Oliver had been born and brought up here. But over the years things changed. Since the couple's retirement to Glenview, their new bungalow, a year earlier, when they'd taken Gennie on as a junior business partner, the only Hammond still living at the pub was Will. And as far as Gennie could see, that was under duress.

Will and his brother couldn't have been more different. Will was twenty-four, almost six feet tall, with a mop of yellowy-blond hair that flopped over intensely blue eyes. He looked and dressed as though he'd just walked off a rugby pitch.

Oliver, in his late twenties, was the elegant one. Taller than Will, but equally broad-shouldered, and with dark hair unexpectedly flecked with grey at the temples. His generous mouth seldom smiled. And it showed no sign of doing so now. To make matters worse, he was watching her.

Gennie forced herself not to look away. She suspected he might be testing her, trying to intimidate her — and she wondered why.

The Hammonds had appointed Will as pub manager, despite Gennie's insistence that she was more than capable of running things on her own.

She now wheeled round to face him. 'Come on, Will. Back me up here. Tell your parents they can't sell the Flying Fox.'

They all turned their attention to Will, and he scowled bad-temperedly at them. 'Do what you like,' he growled. 'You usually do. It's not as if my opinion would actually count for anything.'

Gennie's eyebrow arched. But Will was unrelenting.

'I don't care what you do,' he said wearily.

Out of the corner of her eye she saw Oliver's head come up. His brother's defeatist attitude had surprised him too, but then Will's moods had been erratic this past week.

Gennie put his morose attitude down to his girlfriend, Saffi, having apparently walked out on him. She'd gone two days earlier, without a word to anyone. It had been strange behaviour — even for her. None of the locals knew she'd disappeared, and Gennie wasn't sure any of them would miss her. She felt sorry for the girl. Thinking back now she remembered having to suppress a grin when Molly first set eyes on her.

'Saffi's a Goth, Mum,' Will had explained, as Molly gazed open-mouthed at the vision in black before her.

Gennie was sure she could be a pretty girl if only she would scrape off some of the thick white make-up.

'Pleased to meet you, Mrs Hammond,'

Saffi had mumbled, batting eyelids heavy with mascara. Her dyed auburn hair hung in wispy strands around her pale face.

Molly held her composure and took the girl's hand. She cleared her throat. 'You're not from around here?'

Saffi shook her head. 'No,' she said flatly, obviously intending to reveal no more about herself than was absolutely essential.

Molly turned and raised an eyebrow at Will, which he ignored.

'Saffi is going to help out in the bar, in return for her bed and board.' He gave an embarrassed little cough. 'She'll be sharing with me.'

'Will she now,' Molly said stiffly, eyeing the girl.

Behind Molly's back Gennie gave Saffi an encouraging wink, and she thought she saw the corners of the girl's mouth twitch in acknowledgement.

Molly had turned on her heel and was striding out of the bar, calling over her shoulder as she went, 'Can I have a word with you, Gennie?'

Gennie followed her into the pub's tiny

office. She guessed what was coming. Molly obviously didn't approve of her son's new girlfriend.

'I can't believe he's brought that girl here. What will the locals make of her? She'll drive away what trade we have left.'

'I don't think she's that bad,' Gennie laughed. It was true that Saffi wasn't the best conversationalist she'd ever encountered, but behind the mask of bravado, she suspected the girl was shy.

'She's not going to make small-talk with the customers, is she?' Molly protested. 'Just wait till Mitch hears about this.'

Gennie didn't think Molly was giving the girl a fair chance. You just had to get used to her that was all. But over the next few weeks she began to wonder if maybe Will's mother had been right. Saffi was moody, and made no effort to engage with the locals. All attempts at friendship with the girl had been met with disinterested frowns. It was clear that Saffi Peters trusted no one — with the possible exception of Will.

The first Gennie knew about her

disappearance was when Saffi failed to turn up for her shift behind the bar. When Gennie mentioned it to Will he'd all but snapped her head off.

'Saffi's just gone home for a bit,' he'd growled.

It was as good as telling her to mind her own business.

Gennie was brought back to the present at the sound of Mitch's voice. Without any preamble, he'd launched into his speech. 'The Fox is in trouble,' he said, throwing a hostile glare in Will's direction. 'I've been through the books, and basically . . . well, they're just a nightmare.'

Gennie swallowed. She couldn't believe she was hearing this. The business was solid. It had to be. She'd buried herself in debt to buy into it.

'I think you'd better explain that, Dad,' Oliver said.

Mitch reached for the pile of ledgers in front of him and opened the top one, flicking pages until he found the section he was looking for. Then he jabbed a finger at the neat rows of figures.

7

'These are a disaster. The bar takings are down month on month. The only thing that's making a profit is the food.' He threw a smile in Gennie's direction. 'And that's because Gennie's in charge of that. But as far as the rest goes . . . ' He sighed. ' . . . we might just as well not bother.'

He glanced up at Will, before going on, 'But that's not all. I had Michael Kent, the accountant, here today going over them — and there's money missing.'

Gennie stared at him, wide-eyed. 'There's money missing?'

Molly bit her lip and fixed her eyes on the table.

'What money?' Oliver demanded. 'How much?'

Mitch shrugged and pursed his lips. 'Five thousand, give or take a few pounds.'

Will glared at the faces around the table. 'OK,' he said. 'I know what you're all thinking . . . that this is down to me. Well I'm not taking all the blame.'

He turned to scowl at his father. 'You really dropped me in it, Dad . . . and you, Mum. I never wanted to run the pub. We all know Oliver was your first choice, but he didn't want it, so the responsibility came to me.' He jabbed a thumb at his chest. 'Muggins here . . . '

Gennie could see Oliver shifting irritably in his chair and groaned inwardly. Mitch and Molly knew there was no way Oliver could give up his architect's business. They couldn't expect him to turn his back on his career to run the village pub — not even for them.

'Your mother and I thought the responsibility would do you good,' Mitch reasoned.

'And you just left me to it, didn't you,' Will jibed. 'And now, when the whole thing is going pear-shaped, you're all leaving me to take the blame . . . well, not this time.'

'Maybe Will's right, Mitch,' Molly cut in. 'We did go off on that cruise, leaving him to cope on his own before Gennie came. We should have been here to support him.'

'Do you think I would have gone on any cruise if I'd suspected we'd be in this kind of mess?' Mitch flapped an impatient hand at the ledgers. 'What about it, Will?'

he demanded, his voice rising. 'Can you explain how £5,000 can just disappear into thin air?'

Will shrugged. This missing money was the least of his worries. Saffi had disappeared, and nobody seemed to care. 'I don't know what happened to the money,' he said flatly.

'That's not good enough, Will,' Oliver said. 'We deserve an explanation.'

'Well, I don't have one,' Will returned. 'So you'll just have to be satisfied with that, except to say that I didn't take any money.'

'And we're expected to just take your word for that?'

Gennie wished Oliver had tempered his accusing tone because Will suddenly shot up from the table and made a grab for his brother. But Gennie was quick. Leaping to her feet, she lunged forward, yanking the warring pair apart. She'd never seen Will so angry.

'You can keep your pub,' he shouted. 'You try running it for a change. I'm out of here.'

With that he turned and stormed out of

the room. They heard the front door slam behind him, leaving them all staring after him in shocked silence.

Gennie jumped up. 'I'll go after him. I'm sure he didn't mean all that.'

But Mitch waved her back to her seat. 'Leave him,' he said. 'The boy needs to cool off.'

'You and Oliver were both a bit hard on him,' Molly said.

Mitch shook his head in a slow, defeated movement. 'Maybe you're right, but he has rather dumped us in it.' He took a long shuddering sigh. 'Actually it's worse than that, much worse.' He shook his head again. 'The Flying Fox is finished!'

Mitch's voice had been barely above a whisper and Molly, her eyes shimmering with tears, reached for his hand.

Gennie swallowed the lump in her throat and stole a glance at Oliver, who sat grim-faced, his eyes still on the door.

Suddenly she was angry. Why were they all being so submissive? The Flying Fox was the Hammond family's heritage. How could they even think about letting it go? Wasn't it worth fighting for?

She was reliving that first time she'd walked into the pub. She remembered a bewildering selection of bottles gleaming from the shelf behind the bar. Friendly customers perched on high stools around the bar, nodding a welcome as they nursed their drinks. At one end of the room was an impressive, vast inglenook fireplace, where logs burned and crackled, filling the air with the sweet smell of pine.

Gennie loved the casualness of the mis-matched furniture and the stout oak tables.

It was early, but at the far end she could see tables had been set up for dinner. A few of the candles had been lit for effect, sending a flickering glow around the room. She sniffed the air as enticing aromas wafted through from the kitchen.

The large, jovial-faced man behind the bar came round to greet her. 'Miss Durham, isn't it?'

'Gennie . . . please,' she said, taking the extended hand.

'Well, Gennie.' He smiled. 'I'm Mitch Hammond. Come through and meet the rest of the clan.'

Gennie found herself being shepherded

through a door at the end of the bar, through a steamy kitchen, where a red-faced chef was fussing over pans that bubbled and sizzled on a wide, green Aga.

The family sitting room at the back was homely with two huge squashy brown sofas. A fire crackled in the hearth and at the far end of the room, Gennie could see a table had also been set for supper.

Molly Hammond, a small, neat woman with shiny dark hair, greying at the temples, came forward, holding out her hand. 'Miss Durham.'

'It's Gennie,' her husband corrected.

Mrs Hammond shoved a strand of hair out of her eyes with the back of her hand. 'I'm Molly — and I'm very pleased to meet you, Gennie. Come away and sit down. We don't stand on ceremony at the Fox.' She indicated one of the sofas and settled herself on the other one.

'Now tell me. What makes you want to come all the way out here to work in a village pub?'

Gennie's eyes widened. 'Oh, I'm sorry. I thought Mr Whitburn explained things. I want to do more than work here,

Mrs Hammond . . . err . . . Molly. I want to buy into the place.'

Molly Hammond's eyebrow lifted. 'Do you, now? And why would that be?'

Gennie took a deep breath. She hadn't been expecting this. She loved her job as receptionist at the five-star Willow Park Hotel. But she was trained in hotel management and her real ambition was to have a pub of her own. Buying into this one was the first step on the ladder.

It had been her father's old business partner, Charles Whitburn, who'd told them the owners of the Flying Fox, in rural Yorkshire, were looking for a junior partner. A twenty per cent slice of the business was being offered at a price which, with the help of her parents and an amenable bank manager, Gennie might just be able to afford.

Daniel Durham wasn't sure this was the right investment for his daughter, but Morven had squeezed his hand and given him the kind of look he could never resist.

'This means a lot to our Gennie,' she had coaxed. 'And you know how deter-mined she is. If we don't give her the money she'll only go and borrow it somewhere else with goodness knows what rate of interest.' She patted her husband's hand. 'She has your stubborn streak, my darling.' She could see his resolve was crumbling.

Daniel knew his wife was right, but they were both surprised when Gennie came up with a proposal of her own.

'I have my savings, and I've already made an appointment with my bank manager for a business loan,' she told them. 'But it would be an enormous help if you wanted to invest a little as well,' she ventured coaxingly.

Daniel threw his head back, roaring with laughter, and then opened his arms wide to his daughter. 'Your mother has taught you well, Gennie,' he said, as she ran into his arms.

'You won't regret it Dad . . . really you won't,' she'd said.

So the finance was put in place, and now all Gennie had to do as she stood in the pub's cosy back room, was to satisfy herself that the Flying Fox was the right investment.

She'd squared her shoulders and met

Molly's eyes. 'It's quite simple.' She looked around her. 'I just want to be part of a place like this. Of course, I'd have to see the books and everything.'

'And we'd have to satisfy ourselves that you were the kind of partner to take our business forward,' Molly Hammond said. But there had been a twinkle in her eye.

An hour later, after a whistle-stop tour of the premises, Gennie had been presented with the pub's business ledgers to peruse at her leisure.

'You could have that big front room upstairs,' Molly Hammond said, then hesitated. 'It's only fair to tell you that there might be a problem in the kitchen. Our chef has already given in his notice. He's moving to France, but not for another six weeks.'

Gennie's head was spinning. She'd been totally bowled over by the friendly, homely Flying Fox, and the quaint little village of Fenwick-cum-Marton. She could see herself settling in here very nicely.

She was already letting her heart rule her head. It wasn't until later that she realised she should have given more thought to the business side of things. She'd asked her father and Charles Whitburn to go over the books. They had advised caution, but she had ignored their advice, believing that if she loved the place enough she could make it work.

'It's exactly the sort of business opportunity I've been hoping to find,' she said, her eyes shining as her hand shot out to be heartily shaken by Molly and Mitch Hammond in turn.

Two weeks later she had moved into the pub and was working alongside the chef, Donnie, in the kitchen. By the time he'd left for France, Gennie had put her own homely twist on the menus, and although she wasn't a trained chef she had faith in the local women who helped out in the kitchen. Very gradually the number of covers in the Fox's small restaurant was beginning to increase.

Surely the current problems were just a temporary stumbling block? They couldn't give up on the old pub. She wouldn't allow it. She shot a desperate glance to Oliver. 'Tell them, Oliver! The Fox is as big a part of this family as any one of you.

You can't just give up on it.'

Mitch pursed his lips and tapped the file of ledgers in front of him. 'Much as I've tried, Gennie,' he said wearily, 'I can't see that we have an option.' He managed a weak smile. 'Look, we all appreciate how you feel, but there are no choices left to us. The Flying Fox is losing money hand over fist. We just can't afford to keep it going.'

Gennie saw Molly wince and wished she hadn't spoken so sharply. She knew that this wasn't a step the Hammonds were taking lightly. The pub had been their life, not to mention the beating heart of the village, for the past fifty years.

Why hadn't she seen this coming? She'd been too preoccupied with her own little corner of the business to even notice the bigger picture. Now that she considered it again, the bar had been getting quieter for some time. People were staying at home rather than coming out for a friendly drink in the evenings. But it wasn't just the money thing.

Something seriously wrong had been happening right under her nose that was making the customers stay away.

Mitch's voice cut into her thoughts. 'It might have been different if Oliver was free to take over the reins — '

'You know that's not possible, Dad,' Oliver sighed. 'We've been over this so many times. Things are difficult for all businesses at the moment.' He cleared his throat. 'The Fox isn't the only one that's in trouble.'

'What! Oh, Oliver. Why didn't you say something?' Molly's face was wreathed in concern.

Oliver shrugged. 'I thought we could deal with it.'

'And can't you?' his father interrupted.

'I don't know, it's complicated. We'll have to see.'

Gennie frowned. There had been no hint of this over the past weeks. But then why would he confide in her? It wasn't as if they were close. Oliver wasn't exactly unfriendly to her, but there was a certain reserve, a holding back, that Gennie didn't understand. He was obviously wary of trusting her, and she didn't know why. She suddenly wondered if he resented her being there. But somebody had to do something and none of the others seemed motivated.

She drew in a sharp breath. It was now or never. 'Will you let me have a look at the books, Mitch?'

There was a stunned silence during which the three others exchanged looks.

'But, Gennie dear, Mitch told you . . . the accountants have already done all that,' Molly said.

'Yes, I know, and I'm not questioning their efficiency.' She was getting the first inklings of an idea. 'But surely it's worth checking out even the remotest of possibilities?' She paused. 'We all owe ourselves that much.'

'I didn't realise you were a trained accountant,' Oliver said coolly.

His father shot him a warning look.

Gennie coloured. 'I'm sorry,' she stammered. 'I didn't mean to overstep the mark. I just thought that if I could help . . . ' She was desperately trying to control her rising embarrassment. But then, why shouldn't she be trusted with the business accounts? She was part of the business, for heaven's sake. 'It's only that . . . well I used to do the books for my father's business, and I thought if I could spot something . . . ' Her words trailed off.

Mitch Hammond looked at his wife and she gave him a nod. He smiled. 'Well, why not?' he said, and pushed the ledgers across the table to Gennie.

Out of the corner of her eye she could see Oliver's questioning frown, but she ignored it. She reached for the ledgers, feeling a little twinge of excitement. A plan was beginning to form in her mind. She'd still no idea if she could do it, but she was certainly going to try.

2

Oliver drew Gennie aside as they left the bungalow. She guessed what was coming.

'Could I have a word? Gennie?'

It had been clear from his body language that he wasn't happy about her going over the books. Well, that was just too bad. Twenty per cent of this business was hers and she was already blaming herself for not realizing how badly it was sinking. She'd been so focused on trying to improve the catering she hadn't realised how much other things had deteriorated.

'I should get back,' she said defensively, hugging the ledgers.

'Half an hour of your time, that's all I'm asking,' he said stiffly.

She frowned, glancing at the low-slung sports car parked just beyond the gate of the bungalow. She'd walked up from the pub . . . and the ledgers were getting heavy.

He pounced on her hesitation. 'Come to the cottage for a drink. I'll drive you back to the Fox.'

Oliver had passed up the opportunity of a highly desirable riverside apartment in one of York's converted warehouse developments for the old cottage just a couple of miles out of Fenwick-cum-Marton.

Keeper's Cottage, the 18th-century gamekeeper's lodge, had stood empty since the estate provided a new bungalow for the man. A hundred years ago the whole village had been part of the Fenwick Estate, including the Flying Fox Inn, but over the years the properties had been sold off. Only a few still remained in estate ownership.

In the nine months Gennie had known Oliver, he'd never invited her to his home. Curiosity got the better of her and she gave him a resigned smile. 'Half an hour then, but after that I have to get back. I left Celia in charge and told her I'd be back within the hour.'

'Will's bound to be there by now, so I shouldn't worry,' Oliver said briskly, opening the car door and relieving her of the heavy ledgers.

Another first, thought Gennie as she slid into the low seat, enjoying the masculine leathery smell of the car's interior. She'd seen the dark blue Porsche around the village, but now sitting next to Oliver as they sped through the fading evening light, she was beginning to enjoy herself.

She had imagined Oliver's cottage would be smart and clinical — much like himself — very masculine and full of his architect's straight lines and geometric shapes. She had to stifle the gasp of surprise as she stepped inside the sitting room.

Pale grey walls provided a background for Oliver's collection of Impressionist artwork: Gennie didn't doubt they would be originals, and as such probably expensive. A huge recessed hearth dominated the longest wall and contained a black wood-burning stove that had obviously been lit earlier and was still glowing red.

The light-coloured walls and spaciousness of the room offset the low beamed ceiling. Cosiness was the last thing she had expected of Oliver Hammond, but the room was definitely cosy.

A draughtsman's easel had been set up at the far end displaying some of Oliver's work in progress. He obviously worked a lot from home.

'Take a seat,' he said, moving to a drinks table behind a dark red Chesterfield sofa. The cracks in the leather gave it character, making Gennie suspect that it was probably a pricey antique.

'What would you like to drink?' he called over his shoulder.

'Gin, please, a small one.' She could see him slicing a lemon with a long-bladed knife.

He handed her the drink. He'd splashed in some tonic and she sipped it appreciatively. 'What exactly did you want to talk about, Oliver?'

He'd poured himself a whisky and came to join her, sitting opposite. But before he had a chance to speak she held up her hand. 'Wait! Let me guess. You're not happy about me going through the Flying Fox's books. Exactly what do you think I might find?'

Oliver's brows came together in an annoyed frown. 'What are you talking about? Of course I don't think you're going to find anything suspicious. And I have absolutely no objection to your looking through the books.'

He hesitated. 'It's just that . . . well, this business about Will.' He looked up, his grey eyes meeting her own. 'He didn't take that missing £5,000. I'd stake my life on it.'

It wasn't the response she'd been expecting. She felt herself relax. 'I agree,' she said. 'I can't see your brother dipping into the pub takings.'

Oliver sank back in his chair. 'Well, if we discount you — and I do of course,' he added quickly, 'that only leaves one other person.'

Gennie knew he was talking about Saffi. 'We can't be sure of anything at this stage,' she protested. 'And we certainly can't go around accusing people who are not here to defend themselves. Besides, that's not the reason I asked to see the books.

'I feel partly to blame for all this,' she said. 'I mean, I was right there. I should have realised how much business was falling off, but I was so wrapped up in the kitchen side of things I suppose I just closed my eyes to the rest.'

She released a long, heartfelt sigh. 'I can see I'll have to buck up my ideas. Things need to change, and that starts with a proper business plan.'

Oliver drained his glass and smiled. It wasn't something that Gennie had seen him do very often and it transformed his whole face. He wasn't actually that bad-looking, Gennie thought with a start.

'What we need is a pleasant smile behind the bar, for let's face it, the welcome down there hasn't been exactly warm in recent times.'

She knew he was right. Saffi, with her persistently discontented expression, and total disinclination to engage in conversation with anyone, probably did her bit to chase the customers away. And the stress of the current financial situation hadn't exactly improved Will's people skills.

To be fair though, as far as she could

make out, Mitch and Molly had never actually asked if Will wanted to manage the Flying Fox. Oliver certainly couldn't do it when he had his own business to run. It had obviously been a case of Will taking over, or selling the place. But wasn't that exactly what they were currently considering? Now that she thought about it, surely if the place had been doing all that well they wouldn't have been looking for a business partner in the first place?

Everything had seemed just fine when she bought into the pub. She'd believed it was thriving. She'd been so happy at the prospect of running her own hostelry that she didn't consider things could go wrong. How naïve was that? She knew now, though, that it wasn't enough to produce reasonable food; the ambience of the place also had to be right if the restaurant was going to attract the number of customers the business needed to prosper. And sadly, the right ambience had certainly been lacking at the Flying Fox over recent months.

Gennie allowed her mind to drift back

again to that first time she had stepped into the pub. There had been warmth that hadn't depended on the cheery fire crackling away in that impressive inglenook fireplace. Customers were smiling, chatting, laughing and enjoying themselves. Bottles and glasses gleamed behind the bar; delicious smells drifted from the kitchen. And overseeing it all was the big, affable figure of Mitch Hammond.

Gennie finished her drink and put down her glass, unaware that Oliver had been watching her.

'You're right,' she said. 'The Flying Fox has lost its way. We have to get it back on track.' She was beginning to get an idea now of what must be done. She'd vaguely realised it when she'd asked to take the books, but now there was a new force surging through her. She was sure she could put things right. Mitch and Molly had done their bit, but they were retired now, and she'd no intention of putting them under any further pressure.

It was up to her now — and she could do it!

It was dark when they left the cottage.

All sorts of plans were coming into Gennie's head as Oliver drove them back to the village. Neither of them saw the sidelights of a car that had been parked further up the lane come on — or noticed that they were followed all the way back to Fenwick.

Before they had even reached the Flying Fox Gennie knew something was wrong. Why was the place in darkness?

She glanced at the clock on the dashboard. It wasn't yet nine o'clock, but the pub was all locked up. She heard Oliver curse.

'What the devil is Will playing at?' he scowled, pulling alongside Gennie's car, which was the only other vehicle in the darkened pub car park.

It crossed her mind that if this had happened nine months ago, there would have been a queue of disgruntled regulars banging on the door demanding to get in. But things were very different now. Perhaps there were no customers and that was why Will had closed. But that didn't make sense either. Why would Oliver's brother do that when he knew that every scrap of income was vital to the business's survival?

'Do you have your keys?' Oliver's voice was cold.

Gennie winced. She knew exactly where her keys were. They were inside the building, hanging on a hook behind the kitchen door.

He stared at her in disbelief. 'You went out without your keys?'

'I wasn't expecting the place to be closed when I got back,' she replied hotly. But he was right, of course. She should have taken the keys with her. She just wasn't prepared to admit that to *him*.

He nodded at the car's glove compartment. 'Can you grab the torch in there?'

She did and together they crept around the back of the building, their shoes crunching on the gravel. There were no lights in the living quarters either. Oliver shone his torch through one of the rear windows, but in the darkness they could only make out the vague shapes of bar furniture.

'Are you there, Will?' Gennie called.

31

'Come on, Will. Stop playing silly devils and let us in.'

They both listened, but there was no response.

'He's obviously not here,' Oliver said. He'd taken the torch from Gennie and shone it at the garage doors. 'His car's gone.'

Gennie chewed her lip, trying to remember. 'I don't think he drove himself to your folks' place tonight, so maybe his old Renault is in that garage he uses in Fordham.'

In the torchlight she saw Oliver's doubtful stare.

'Well, it's always breaking down,' she reasoned, trying to recall if Will had mentioned such a thing earlier. She wasn't sure, and sighed. 'OK, so he's not here, is he?'

They tramped round the back of the building. The curtains in the sitting room were open and she peered in for any sign of a light inside the building, but there was nothing. She remembered how angry Will had been after his spat with Oliver earlier. What if he had come back in a rage and left the hatch door to the cellar open? It would be so easy to tumble down those steps. A shiver ran down Gennie's spine. What if Will was lying down there, injured?

She walked back round to the front and made one last desperate attempt to call for him. 'For heaven's sake, Will, it's me . . . Gennie. If you're there just open the door.'

No response.

She went back to where Oliver stood. He was moving the torch around, scanning the building for a way in. Suddenly he stopped, flashing the beam of light upwards. 'Look . . . up there . . . is that window open?'

He trained the light at the top of the back porch. There was a tiny gap, but too small for either of them to squeeze through.

'I've an idea,' he said, thrusting the torch into Gennie's hand. 'Hold this. I'll just be a minute.'

Gennie heard the crunch of his shoes as he crossed to his car and the clunk of the boot closing after he'd retrieved what he was looking for.

'It's the belt from my coat,' he explained. 'If I can dangle it through and catch the latch of the big window . . . '

After a few futile attempts, the buckle caught on the window latch and with one firm tug it came free of its hook. Oliver dug his nails down the side of the window and it swung open.

'Well done,' Gennie whispered.

A few minutes later they were creeping through the Flying Fox like a couple of guilty intruders.

Gennie found the light switch and they checked around the bar and kitchen. Everything seemed normal. They went upstairs into Will and Saffi's room.

'I've a feeling we shouldn't be here,' Oliver said.

But Gennie knew she couldn't rest until she was satisfied that Will wasn't here. Her hand went to her mouth when she saw the disarray inside the room. Clothes had been dragged from the wardrobe and heaped on the bed. A suitcase lay open and abandoned on the floor.

'Looks like Will has packed a few things

and gone,' said Oliver, his face grim.

Gennie checked the other wardrobe. It was full of Saffi's clothes, all neatly draped on hangers. Gennie ran a hand over the black and grey garments. She turned to Oliver, her eyes wide. 'Saffi hasn't taken her clothes . . . why would she leave without her clothes?' She turned, heading for the stairs. 'I'm going to get to the bottom of this. Can you hang on here a bit longer, Oliver?'

He nodded. 'Where are you going?'

'I need to see Celia. She must have been here when Will got back. She's bound to know what's happened.'

'I'll come with you.'

'No,' she said. 'You stay here. She might feel intimidated if we both turn up demanding answers.'

'OK, but don't you get lost too, will you?' he called after her.

'I'll be fine,' Gennie shouted back. 'Celia's place is just five minutes away.'

She hurried up the back street, past the terraced cottages until she reached the solid grey granite house that stood on its own. The lights were on in the downstairs room and Gennie knocked at the door. She could hear hesitant footsteps on the other side as Celia decided if it was safe to open the door to an unexpected night-time caller.

'It's me . . . Gennie,' she called through the letterbox.

The door opened and Celia peered out at her.

'Sorry to call so late, Celia, but — '

Celia opened the door wider and waved her into the narrow hall, indicating she should go through to the front room. 'No guesses as to why you're here,' she said, following her through. 'I told him not to shut the pub. I knew you wouldn't be pleased. But you know how hot-headed he can be these days.'

'Do you mean Will? But I don't understand. Why did he close the pub? The whole place is locked up and in darkness — and there's no sign of him.'

Celia shrugged. 'I've no idea.' She paused, thinking back. 'We only had two customers in all the time you were all away up the hill at your meeting. And no food orders at all. I could tell Will was in a foul mood when he came back.

' 'That's it Celia,' he said. 'We're not sitting around here all night twiddling our thumbs. You get off home. We'll have an early night for once.' '

'He said what?' Gennie's voice rose. 'But he had no right to do that.'

'It wasn't down to me . . . you understand that?' The woman was looking worried now. 'I left the kitchen sparkling. There wasn't any mess.'

Gennie put her hand on the older woman's arm. 'I'm not blaming you, Celia. You just did what you were told. But have you any idea where Will went?'

'You mean he's not in the pub?'

Gennie shook her head.

'Well, no. I've no idea where he is. He didn't say he was going out, or anything.'

'OK, Celia. That's fine. He'll turn up in his own good time.' She was trying to sound as casual as she could. 'Did you happen to notice if his car was in the car park when you left?'

'Well, the garage doors were closed, but I assumed it was in there.'

Gennie nodded on her way to the door.

37

'Sorry for disturbing you.'

'He's not gone and disappeared, has he?' Celia called after her as she hurried out to the street.

'Of course not. He'll be playing cards with some of his mates.' Gennie tried to sound unconcerned, but she knew Celia would not be fooled. Here was a bit of local intrigue ... some juicy gossip — and it would be all round the village by first light.

In her absence, Oliver had collected the Flying Fox's business ledgers from his car and left them on the kitchen table. He'd also made a pot of coffee and was lifting two mugs from their hooks when Gennie burst back in, breathless. 'Seems Will has just taken off in a temper,' she said, collapsing onto a chair. She retold Celia's story, and watched as Oliver's expression grew grimmer.

'Maybe he's gone after Saffi,' he suggested.

'Maybe ... ' Gennie was thoughtful. 'But that doesn't explain why her clothes are all still upstairs.'

Oliver poured the coffees and they drank them in silence.

When they had finished she asked in a quiet voice, 'Should we call the police?' She could see the muscles working in Oliver's jaw. He was obviously as worried as she was.

'No, not yet. Let's wait until morning. Will might have come back by then.' He looked up and met her eyes. 'I'll sleep upstairs in that spare room tonight. I don't want you staying here on your own, Gennie.'

'But I'll be fine,' she protested.

'Even so.'

Inside her chest, her heart was pounding. Much as she loved the Flying Fox, she had not been looking forward to spending the night here alone. But the thought of Oliver sleeping just through the wall sent a sudden tingle up her spine. She took a deep breath. 'It really isn't necessary,' she said, mentally crossing her fingers that he wouldn't take her at her word.

'I think it is,' he said firmly. 'Fancy a nightcap before getting your head down?'

Gennie didn't, but she followed him through to the bar and watched as he held a glass to the whisky optic, then smiled as she saw him leave money on the bar top.

In the back room she sank gratefully onto the sofa, while Oliver took the one opposite. Then he jumped . . . his head jerked up.

'I thought I heard something?' His eyes were instantly alert.

Gennie listened, and then shook her head. 'All I can hear is the wind.'

But Oliver was on his feet. 'Better make sure. You stay here,' he ordered, striding towards the pub's back door. A second later and he would have missed seeing the red tail-lights swing out of the Flying Fox's car park as the vehicle's driver headed out of the village at speed. It could just have been a customer taking off when he found the pub closed. But Oliver knew that it wasn't. His heart was pumping. He paused to calm his breathing before going back.

Gennie looked up, smiling when he came in.

'You were right,' he said. 'It was probably the wind.'

He settled back on the sofa and reached for his glass. He knew who was driving that car.

Gennie was exhausted when she finally crawled into bed that night and was asleep almost as soon as her head hit the pillow. In her dream someone was pounding on her bedroom door. 'Gennie . . . Wake up Gennie! I have to go!'

She shook herself awake, but the pounding persisted. Then she realised it was no dream. It was Oliver! And there was panic in his voice. She jumped up and, without reaching for a dressing gown, threw open her door.

Oliver was on the landing, fully dressed, his face ashen. 'It's Dad,' he said. 'He's had a heart attack. Mum's just rung me from the hospital.'

Gennie's eyes flew open, and her hand went out instinctively to touch his arm. 'Oh, Oliver. I'm so sorry.' Her head was in a whirl. 'What can I do? Do you know how serious it is?' She searched his face for an answer, but Oliver only shook his head.

'I don't know any more than I've told

41

you, but Mum's in a terrible state. I'm going there now.'

'I'm coming with you,' Gennie said, turning to grab her clothes. But he stopped her.

'No. I'll get there faster if I leave now; besides, you need to stay and look after this place. You can come along later, if you like.'

'Of course.' She nodded. 'You must go. Molly will need you.'

But he had already turned and was striding along the corridor.

'Give them both my love,' she called after him, as he took the stairs two at a time.

3

Sleeping was out of the question after Oliver left. Gennie glanced at the clock. It was five-thirty. She reached for her white towelling robe and went barefoot downstairs to the kitchen. Her head was all over the place. She made herself a cup of instant coffee and sat staring into it. She was annoyed with herself for not insisting on going with Oliver to the hospital. The Hammonds were like family to her. She should be there with them now, helping Oliver to comfort his mother.

And Will! Where was he? Would he turn up shamefaced and full of remorse for having taken off in such an irresponsible way? If he didn't come back, his disappearance would make the situation so much worse for Molly. She ran her fingers through her short fair hair and shook her head. Yesterday everything had been normal — well, as normal as it could be considering Saffi had gone. First

Saffi and now Will! Had they planned it this way? Mitch had said £5,000 was missing. A couple could get quite far away with that amount of cash.

She screwed up her face and dismissed the idea as soon as it crossed her mind. Will would never do anything so underhand and, although she didn't know his girlfriend very well, from what she'd seen of the girl, she'd seemed honest enough. So where were they?

She reached for her coffee. It was stone cold and she went to tip it down the sink. Outside the first fingers of light were beginning to sneak across the sky. In six hours' time she would have to open the pub. She'd no idea what the rest of the day would bring.

Gennie went back upstairs to shower and dress, taking time to check her mobile, but there was no missed message from Oliver. Maybe that was a good sign, but an update would have been welcome. She stared at the silent phone. The only way she was going find out about Mitch was to go to the hospital herself. York was a forty-minute drive away, probably even quicker at this time of day. She'd already checked that the bar was stocked and ready for the day's business, and then went round the building checking everything was secure. Celia had a key to the premises that she could use in emergencies, so Gennie knew she could ring her to open up if she was delayed getting back.

Oliver and his mother were sitting in a corridor outside the hospital's intensive care unit when Gennie arrived. They looked up as she hurried in. Molly managed a weak smile.

'How is he?' Gennie asked breathlessly.

'No change,' Oliver said, and the worry in his eyes made Gennie's heart contract.

A tall, grey-haired man with spectacles emerged from the ward's double doors. The three of them sprang to their feet, fixing him with anxious stares.

He shook his head, his expression kindly. 'No news yet, I'm afraid.' And at the sight of the despondent faces, added, 'But that's not necessarily a bad thing. Mitch is holding his own at the moment.'

He smiled and touched Molly's hand.

'Try not to worry too much.'

'Can I see my husband?'

'Of course, but just for a few minutes. After that I suggest you let your son take you home for a few hours' rest. There's nothing you can do here, and we will be in touch the moment there is any change in your husband's condition.'

Oliver sighed as he watched his mother go through the double doors. 'It was good of you to come, Gennie.'

She swallowed, before saying quietly, 'Is there anything I can do, Oliver? I feel so helpless.'

He turned suddenly towards her, and to Gennie's amazement, tilted back her chin and looked searchingly into her eyes. 'You do care, don't you?' he said in a voice full of emotion.

Gennie desperately tried to blink back the tears, but they rolled down her cheeks, anyway. He brushed them away with his fingers.

'Dad's a fighter,' he said, gently. 'He'll come through this.'

But she didn't hear his silent plea. 'He must come through it . . . for all our sakes,' he prayed.

Oliver was remembering the look that had shot between his parents when he announced all those years ago that he wanted to be an architect. He knew they had hoped he would eventually take over the running of the Flying Fox and use his flair to build it into an even more successful business than they ever could. Had he been selfish to pursue his own career dreams? If so, then he was certainly getting his comeuppance now.

Brian Wells, Oliver's business partner, seemed set on destroying everything the pair of them had built up over the past six years. The man's interest in their company, Hammond Wells Associates, seemed to have plunged to an all-time low. It was a regular occurrence now for Brian to turn up late for important meetings, and he always had an excuse when tight schedules over-ran — as they seemed to do rather a lot these days, Oliver thought grimly. There was a limit, though, to the number of times you could let a client down before they became an ex-client.

Brian's drinking was making him careless. It would only take one tiny calculation out of place for an entire multi-million-pound development to collapse around their ears. Oliver had nightmares about the kind of chaos that could cause.

And then there was Laura . . . willowy, elegant, beautiful Laura. She and Brian had been married for ten years, but the child they longed for just hadn't happened. Maybe that was the problem . . . maybe it had nothing to do with him. But he knew he was wrong. If he'd never introduced them to Sophie, all of their lives might be very different now.

Oliver had been captivated from the first moment he'd set eyes on the vivacious redhead. Sophie Chandler was PA to the chief executive of a Manchester advertising agency. They'd met when he and Brian designed the company's new office building. He sighed, his eyes clouding over as he remembered.

Sophie was like an exotic butterfly, a party girl who loved the bright lights. And for a while that suited Oliver. He was mixing with a whole new set of people and in the beginning he'd found their company exhilarating. They worked hard and played hard — and provided his business with a lot of new contacts.

Brian and Laura were mesmerised by Sophie. The three of them became inseparable, like peas in a pod. Even when Oliver had other engagements and couldn't join them, they were quite happy to go out together without him.

Oliver had been smitten with Sophie, but in his heart he knew it was not love. How could you love someone who cheated on you? But still, she was vibrant and funny, and he'd been very fond of her.

Even now he could feel his blood running cold at the thought of his beautiful Sophie, her body bloodied and bloated, floating face-down in the River Ouse. She'd been stabbed to death! The memory of those dark days still had the power to send icy chills surging through his veins.

Brian and Laura had appeared inconsolable. Oliver hadn't realised the three of them had become so close. At first he'd assumed they just liked partying together, but more than once he'd caught a certain look passing between Brian and Sophie. There was no proof that his partner and his girlfriend had been lovers. But he knew it in his bones. He just knew! It had been about then that Brian's drinking had started.

Sophie's murder had shocked everyone. The locals in Fenwick-cum-Marton didn't know her, but they knew the Hammonds, and word soon spread when police questioned Oliver about the killing. The subsequent search of his cottage and removal of Sophie's belongings in plastic evidence bags caused a sensation in the village, even though officers admitted there was no evidence against him.

All that had been two years ago now, and the police seemed no further forward in finding the killer.

Gennie had been watching Oliver staring into space, and flinched when she saw the dark shadow come over his eyes. She suspected that whatever worries he had been going over in his mind were far away from this hospital. But that was none of her business. She cleared her throat. 'Any word from Will?'

Her voice seemed to come from a long way off and Oliver's head jerked up. He was annoyed with himself for allowing the dark memories to surface again. The past was the past. This was what he must focus on now — this bleak corridor, and his father fighting for his life just a few feet away.

His stare was like granite. 'Will?' He hesitated, steadying his thoughts. 'Oh, no . . . nothing yet. His mobile is switched off. I can't see any other way of contacting him.'

Gennie bit her lip. 'How much does your mum know about last night?'

'Only that Will has gone away. She thinks he's off looking for that girlfriend of his, and is just out of touch.' Oliver grimaced. 'I didn't mention that I'm going to kill him when he does get back.'

Gennie looked up and gave him a wry grin. 'You're probably right. I think he's gone off to find Saffi. I'll have a look around and see if I can find a contact address for her when I get back.'

'That would be a help. Thanks.'

He saw her glance up at the clock. 'You should make a move. You've got a pub to run, remember?' His smile was fleeting.

She got up to leave, then stopped. 'What about Molly?'

'I'll look after her. You get back to Fenwick. I'll call if there's any news here.'

It was almost ten o'clock when Gennie drove into the pub car park. She was just about to put her key in the back door when she heard someone calling her name. She turned. 'Caro! Am I pleased to see you! Have you time to come in for a coffee?'

'Make that tea, and I'm all yours,' her friend laughed.

Spirited, dark-haired, and full of fun, Caroline Dent was unlike any vicar's wife Gennie had ever known. But then her husband, Tom, wasn't your run-of-the-mill vicar either. They'd come to Fenwick six months earlier, and although the Hammond family — with the exception of Will — would be sitting in the pews of St Stephen's Church every Sunday, not more than a handful of other villagers had ever bothered.

But that was before the word got round that the Rev Tom Dent was a preacher with a difference. In the pulpit he was lively and entertaining. He also took the trouble to get to know his parishioners, and used their names affectionately in his sermons, just as he would have done if he'd met them in the street.

Not long after they moved in Caro asked for Gennie's help to start a Parents and Toddlers' Group. A playgroup was also established and now both were a rousing success with children attending from all the surrounding villages.

Tom's predecessor, the Rev Cedric White, was a kindly man, but he and his wife, Mildred, had more of an eye on retirement than immersing themselves in village life. So the church hall grew silent and most of the community groups had gradually disbanded. Everyone agreed that Caro and Tom had breathed new life into Fenwick-cum-Marton.

'Come on in,' Gennie said, stepping into the pub kitchen and dumping her bag on the nearest worktop. 'I'll stick the kettle on.'

But Caro caught her hand and made her sit down. 'Now,' she said, her dark eyes full of concern, 'tell me what Will's been playing at.'

Gennie shook her head, laughing. 'It didn't take Celia long to spread the word.'

'Never mind her. Just tell me what's going on — and how I can help.'

As Caro busied herself with the tea things, Gennie recounted the previous night's events, finishing with the shock news about Mitch's heart attack.

Cara's hand went to her mouth. 'Oh, my word. Poor Molly. But how is Mitch? Have you heard?'

Gennie's shoulders slumped. 'He's quite poorly. But Oliver is there with them.'

Caro nodded.

'When did all this happen?'

'Oliver got a call from his mum at five-thirty this morning and went straight to the hospital. I joined them there later, but I had to come back to open this place.' She sighed. 'The doctors have

54

advised Molly to come home and get a few hours' rest, but she won't hear of it. She's insisting on staying with Mitch.'

Caro was silent for a moment then her hand slapped the table. 'Right. What you need is some practical help around here. How would you fancy having another barmaid?'

Gennie laughed. 'Are you offering?'

'I certainly am. You can give me a crash course in bar skills and how your till works, etc., then I'll be good to go.'

'But, Caro — '

'No buts! I'll just nip back to the vicarage to put Tom in the picture and then I'll be right back.'

Gennie threw her arms around her friend's neck. 'You've no idea how much I appreciate this, Caro. You're a real lifesaver. It means I can get back to the hospital later to give the others a break. Maybe Molly could even be persuaded to come home if she's assured that one of us will stay with Mitch.'

While Caro was away Gennie busied herself making sandwiches for the bar. Once word got round about Mitch, they were bound to be busy. The Hammonds were popular in the village and the locals were sure to call in for the latest news on his health.

Gennie had put up a notice explaining that the restaurant would be temporarily closed. It hadn't taken long for the news to spread and a steady stream of customers — some clutching Get Well cards — came and went. Gennie worked alongside Caro in the bar until lunchtime.

'You should get off to the hospital. Now that I've got the hang of this, I'll manage fine.'

'Are you sure?'

'Of course I am. If it gets really busy I can always call on Celia. Give them all my love. That goes for Tom too,' she called after Gennie, as she went to collect her jacket from the kitchen. 'In fact you might see him up there. He said he would try to look in at the hospital.'

Gennie dropped the cards into her bag as she ran out the back door to her car.

The smile that spread across Oliver's face when he caught sight of her made Gennie's heart do a little flip. He looked genuinely pleased to see her.

'What's the latest?' she asked breathlessly, taking the seat next to him.

'No change, I'm afraid. Mum's in there with Dad now. They let her have a few minutes by his bedside when she really pleads with them.'

'You look shattered,' Gennie said.

'I'm fine,' he said stiffly. 'It's Mum I'm worried about. She's been here for ten hours, and not slept a wink. She won't eat anything, either.'

'Molly's strong. She'll be fine. They both will.' But her fingers were tightly crossed.

When Molly emerged from the ward, Gennie had to stifle a gasp of shock. She almost didn't recognise her for she looked so deathly pale, and the lack of sleep had produced dark smudges, almost like bruises, under her eyes. Gennie jumped up and went to her, arms wide. Gently she led Molly back to Oliver, and then sat down beside her.

'These are for Mitch,' she said, fishing in her bag for the bundle of Get Well cards their friends had left. 'Everyone sends their love. Caro is looking after the pub, so I can stay just as long as you need me.'

Molly took the cards and stared at them. Huge tears began to roll down her cheeks. It was the first time she'd wept since that awful moment when she woke during the night to find Mitch next to her, clutching his chest. She made no attempt to stop the flow. 'You're all being so kind to us,' she whispered shakily.

Gennie had to force back her own tears. 'That's because we all love you . . . you and Mitch.'

Molly patted her hand. 'Thank you,' she said quietly. Then, after a pause, 'I don't suppose you've heard from Will?'

Gennie shook her head and glanced at Oliver. 'I think you should let Oliver take you home. It will do you good to get away from here for a few hours and take some rest.'

'I have a better idea,' Molly said, turning to her son. 'Now that Gennie is here with me there is no need for you to stay, Oliver. I know you're worried about that business of yours.'

Oliver opened his mouth to protest, but

his mother waved away his objection. 'I've seen you going off and talking into that mobile phone. I think you should go along to your office . . . just to satisfy yourself that things are running smoothly in your absence.'

'That's a really good idea, Oliver,' Gennie agreed.

He looked from one to the other, unsure what to do.

'It's not negotiable, darling,' Molly said, sending a mischievous grin to Gennie. 'Did I use the right phrase?'

Gennie giggled. 'Sounds about right to me. You don't seem to be left with an option, Oliver.'

'Well, OK,' he agreed hesitantly. 'But only if you're sure. I'll be back in just over an hour.'

Both women nodded and he kissed his mother's cheek. Just for a second, Gennie wondered if he would also kiss her. But he didn't.

Molly smiled forlornly after him. 'Poor Oliver. He has so much pressure on him at the moment.'

'Really?' Gennie remembered he had

hinted at things not being right with his business when they held the family conference. Had that only been the previous evening? So much had happened since then.

Molly nodded. 'His business partner is giving him a difficult time.' She pursed her lips. 'And then there's that wife of his.'

Gennie raised an eyebrow, encouraging more information.

'She's the cause of all the trouble,' Molly said, and then paused. 'I just hope Oliver is not having an affair with her.'

Gennie froze. An affair! Why did the thought of that send chills down her spine? In fact, why was she even thinking about Oliver when it was his mother who needed her support?

She straightened up. 'Have you eaten anything today, Molly?'

The older woman shook her head. 'I'm not hungry.'

'That's not what I asked,' Gennie said firmly. 'You have to keep your strength up. Mitch is going to need you when he comes round.'

A sudden gleam of hope sprang into

Molly's eyes. 'Do you think so? Do you really believe that, Gennie?'

'Of course I do, and so should you. Now, how about that sandwich?'

Molly gave a reluctant nod. 'But I'm not promising I'll be able to eat it.'

But when Gennie returned with two chicken and salad sandwiches on wholemeal bread, Molly found she was ravenous.

'You were right,' she said, taking a tissue from her bag and dabbing her mouth. 'I needed that.' She turned to face Gennie. 'Now, tell me about Will. Where the devil is he? He should be here.'

The mention of Oliver's errant brother took Gennie by surprise. She had no more of an idea where Will was than any of them, but she didn't want to upset Molly. With Mitch so ill she had enough to worry about.

The arrival of Tom Dent, flushed and bright-eyed from having run up two flights of stairs rather than wait for the hospital elevator, saved further explanation about Will.

'Molly,' he said, his voice gentle. 'How

61

are you bearing up?'

'I'm fine, Tom. It's Mitch who needs your prayers.' Her eyes slid to the closed doors of the ICU opposite. 'There's still no change.' She paused. 'They seem to think that's not a bad thing.'

'She needs to go home and get some sleep, Tom,' Gennie interrupted. 'Maybe she will listen to you.'

'I have a plan,' Tom said.

They both looked at him.

'You permit me to drive you home right now, Molly. You can get your head down for a few hours, and then have a nice shower and a change of clothes. I'll come back to collect you early this evening and bring you back to the hospital.' He took a breath. 'Well, how does that sound?'

'What if Will turns up and I'm not here? I don't want to miss him.'

Tom and Gennie looked at each other.

'I'm sure he'll wait for you,' Tom said.

Molly sighed. 'This is all Will's fault. If he hadn't upset his father so much last night then this might never have happened. And now he has just disappeared . . . '

Gennie's teeth caught at her bottom lip

and she studied the floor. She didn't know what to say.

Finally Molly's shoulders lifted in a shrug and she said, 'All right, I'll come with you, Tom, but let me go through and tell Mitch when I'll be back.'

Tom smiled. 'Good idea,' he said.

'How did you manage that?' Gennie asked, amazed when Molly had disappeared into Mitch's ward.

'Just my touch of genius,' he joked. 'By the way, I called in on my way here to see how Caro was getting on in her new job as your barmaid.'

'And?'

'I think she's missed her vocation. She was loving every minute of it. The bar was pretty busy, but she and Celia seemed to be coping well.'

'Celia was there?'

Tom nodded. 'Caro rang her when more customers came in. I think she made more sandwiches.'

'Right,' said Gennie. Maybe Oliver was right when he said what was needed to bring the customers back to the Flying Fox was a happy face behind the bar. It was a pity Caro couldn't be a permanent fixture.

'I told Mitch I would be back later,' Molly said, emerging from the double doors. 'I think he understood. Are you sure you don't mind staying here on your own, Gennie?'

'Absolutely not, but I was just thinking. I have to get back to the pub once Oliver comes back, but I'll be returning this evening. Perhaps I could collect you from home, Molly, instead of Tom.'

'Well it suits me, if you're sure.'

'No problem. I'll call for you about seven then.' Gennie smiled.

She checked her phone after they'd gone in case she had missed a call from Oliver. He'd been gone for more than two hours. She'd noticed a coffee machine when she went for the sandwiches and wondered if she could find it again.

She needn't have worried. It was situated at the end of the next corridor. As she waited for the plastic cup to fill she glanced through the window to the car park below. Oliver's car was easy to spot. She followed it all the way through the lines of parked vehicles and watched as he pulled into a vacant space.

Another vehicle caught her eye. The small red sports car tore up the lanes at speed, turning into another empty space two down from Oliver's car. Gennie was intrigued and gazed down with some amusement as a tall blonde in an elegant cream suit uncurled herself from the driver's seat of the sports car and slammed the door. Oliver had also emerged and the two met head-on. They exchanged words. Gennie's eyes widened in surprise as the blonde stretched up and kissed Oliver on the mouth.

4

By the time Oliver joined her Gennie had managed to convince herself that his private life was no concern of hers.

'Everything all right at the office?' She slid him a sideways glance.

'Fine, yes.'

But his stony expression told a different story. The encounter with the demonstrative blonde woman in the car park hadn't seemed to improve his mood.

She took a breath. 'Tom Dent stopped by, and managed to talk Molly into having a breather at home for a couple of hours.'

'Really?' His face lit up. 'That *is* good news.'

'And I actually persuaded her to eat a sandwich.'

'Maybe I should go away more often,' he said. 'And before you ask, the answer is *No*. Will still hasn't been in touch.'

He sat down next to her and she

realised he was still wearing the same clothes as yesterday. Then she remembered that he hadn't been home since that early-morning call from Molly to the Flying Fox.

'Will's disappearance has taken a back seat with all this worry over Dad,' he said.

Gennie's brow furrowed. She'd meant to search for Saffi's address back at the pub, but there just hadn't been time.

She was still thinking about that kiss in the car park. She jumped up. 'I'll have to go. I left Caro in charge of the bar and it's lunchtime. I have to get back to check everything's is OK.'

Gennie knew her words were sharper than she'd intended, but from the way Oliver was looking at her she guessed he was putting that down to stress. Maybe he was right. At any rate he nodded as though he'd understood.

She turned to go, and then remembered. Looking back, she said, 'Oh, and I've arranged to pick Molly up at the bungalow at seven this evening and drive her back here.'

'I can do that,' Oliver suggested. 'I'll

collect you, too, if you like. I need to nip home for a shower and change anyway.'

Gennie avoided his eyes. 'Well, if you like . . . thanks, I'd appreciate that.'

On the drive back to Fenwick her mind kept drifting back to the glamorous blonde. She was annoyed that it was bothering her so much. It wasn't as though there was a relationship between her and Oliver Hammond. Until recent events she couldn't even have claimed a friendship. He'd always seemed so distant.

He wasn't a regular customer at the Flying Fox, although lately he had taken to calling in for a bar meal in the evenings. The only thing she could read into that was that it was preferable to cooking for himself when he got back to the cottage.

Once, she remembered, he had turned up with a young woman. She could have been a girlfriend, but Gennie hadn't thought so. The body language was wrong. They were easy enough in each other's company, but there was no meaningful eye contact, no touching of hands.

And now — if his mother was right — here he was having an affair with a married woman. Not just any woman, but the wife of his business partner. Probably the woman she'd seen him kissing earlier. Gennie wondered if the man knew about the affair. If he did then it might explain the friction at work that Molly had also mentioned.

Her mobile rang as she drove into the pub car park. Her hand shook as she reached into her bag for it. Was it news from the hospital? But it was Caro's cheerful voice she heard.

'Just to put your mind at rest, everything went well at lunchtime. All the glasses have been washed and the tables wiped. Everything is now securely locked up.' There was a pause. 'I think I'm getting the hang of this.'

Gennie could hear the smile in her friend's voice. 'Any chance of a repeat performance this evening? I was planning to go back to the hospital with Oliver and Molly.'

'Just try stopping me,' Caro said. 'I'll come over about six-thirty. I still have the key.'

'Thanks, Caro. I owe you.'

Her friend hadn't exaggerated about leaving the bar in ship-shape condition and, since the restaurant was still closed, there was nothing for Gennie to do but relax in a scented bath.

She went upstairs and turned on the taps, tipping a glug of lavender oil into the water. The fragrance was sharp and clean and she breathed it in, already enjoying the essential oil's relaxing qualities. She felt like a new woman half an hour later when she stepped out of the bath and wrapped herself in a white fluffy towel.

She wondered what Molly was doing at that moment and a sudden wave of sadness swept over her. She knew what a happy marriage Mitch and Molly had. He just had to recover . . . he just had to. Recalling the gloomy atmosphere as the three of them had waited earlier in that hospital corridor, Gennie decided a more positive attitude was required. Some faith was needed. It was time all of them started believing in Mitch's strength to fight his way through this.

With that in mind, Gennie flicked

through the dresses in her wardrobe, and selected one of soft blue wool that picked out the flecks of sapphire in her grey eyes. She took care with her make-up and brushed her blonde hair until it shone. When she looked at her image in the mirror, she was already feeling better.

★ ★ ★

Caro arrived early and had gone to busy herself in the bar. She looked up, surprised, when Oliver walked in.

'I'm not a customer,' he assured her, when he saw her flustered expression. 'Just waiting to collect Gennie for the hospital.'

'How *is* Mitch?' Caro asked, her large, dark eyes full of compassion.

'I rang the ward just before I left home. No change in his condition. He still hasn't woken up.'

Caro touched his arm. 'Your father will rally, I'm sure of it. Tom and I are both praying for him.'

In a spontaneous gesture, Oliver reached across the bar and placed a light kiss on Caro's cheek.

She flushed at the unexpected gesture.

Neither of them saw the face at the window. And they didn't hear the quiet clunk of a car door, or the sound of the vehicle moving slowly away and out of the Flying Fox car park.

★ ★ ★

Gennie could have been mistaken, but she thought she saw a glint of approval in Oliver's eyes as she walked into the room. He too had taken trouble with his appearance and looked relaxed in a dark tweed jacket and jeans. She had only ever seen him in formal clothes and decided that this new look suited him.

Molly had been watching for them, and was already out of the front door and hurrying along the path to meet them before Oliver had even climbed out of the driving seat. Gennie was pleased to note that the worrying dark smudges beneath Molly's eyes were beginning to recede. The strain of the past hours was still evident, but she looked more relaxed.

'Did you manage to get any sleep?'

Gennie asked, leaning across to greet the new arrival as her son helped her into the front passenger seat.

'A little, I think, but I couldn't settle. I just need to be with Mitch.'

'Of course you do,' Gennie said gently.

'We'll be there in no time, Mum,' Oliver said.

The ICU was on the second floor and they took the lift, turning left into the now-familiar corridor. A nurse was hurrying towards them. Gennie's heart started to pound. 'Please don't let this be bad news,' she prayed.

The nurse went straight to Molly. 'I'm so glad you've arrived. You're just in time. Come with me.'

Gennie and Oliver exchanged uneasy looks as the nurse propelled Molly through the double doors and into the ward where Mitch lay unconscious.

'Oh, God,' Oliver said, his face turning grey. 'I hope this isn't bad news.'

They walked slowly into the ward, stopping at the sight of Molly by her husband's bed. The man who lay there, pale and still, was nothing like the jovial landlord

Gennie had met on her first visit to the Flying Fox. And then it happened! Mitch's eyelids fluttered.

'There,' the nurse said triumphantly. 'Did you see that? I thought he was coming round. I'm so glad you got here in time to be with him when he woke up.'

Mitch's eyelids fluttered again, and then fully opened as he focused on his wife.

Gennie bit her lip as the tears pricked her eyes. Mitch was waking up! He was going to get better!

She turned to look at Oliver and saw the lump in his throat.

Molly moved forward and gently took Mitch's hand. 'Welcome back, my love,' she whispered.

Mitch's eyes moved round the room and came to rest on his son.

'Good to have you back, Dad,' Oliver said, his voice distinctly croaky.

'That goes for me, too,' Gennie said.

A contented smile had started to spread over Mitch Hammond's face.

The nurse began to check the equipment around the patient's bed. 'Yep, all fine,' she announced with a rueful grin. 'You gave us all quite a scare.'

Mitch, obviously confused, and still trying to find his voice, nodded.

'I think your parents need some time on their own,' she said quietly to Oliver, as she left the ward.

'Of course.' Oliver smiled, putting an arm around Gennie's shoulder and shepherding her into the corridor.

Gennie, trembling with relief and emotion, turned to Oliver, her eyes shining. 'Oh, Oliver. I'm so glad — '

She didn't get to finish the sentence because Oliver had gathered her into his arms and was kissing her.

Gennie's heart was pounding again, but in a very different way, as they drew apart, breathless.

'I'm so sorry, Gennie. I shouldn't have done that.'

She gave a nervous giggle. 'Kissing me wasn't that bad, was it?'

Then, seeing his brows draw together in confusion, she added, 'Don't worry, I understand. It was just the euphoria of the moment.'

'Yes. That's what it was,' he said slowly.

They sat in awkward silence, a chair apart, until Molly joined them, her face wreathed in smiles. 'The nurse says I can sleep here in the relatives' room tonight, so you two can get off if you want.'

They got up. 'We'll just say goodnight to Dad,' Oliver said.

Gennie followed him into the ward, pleased to see that some colour had begun to creep back into Mitch's face.

'Thank everyone for the cards,' he managed in a whispery voice, his eyes sliding to the crowded display on the bedside cabinet.

'I'll call back in the morning, Dad,' Oliver said. Father and son nodded to each other and Gennie could see the emotion in their eyes.

A few minutes later they were driving out of the hospital grounds. Oliver slowed the car at the gates and turned to her. 'Have you eaten?'

She wrinkled her brow, remembering that she hadn't. 'Well . . . no, actually.'

'Me neither,' he said. 'Allow me to buy you supper.'

'That would be lovely,' she replied demurely.

'If you fancy Italian food, I know a nice little place just off the ring road.'

'Sounds great.'

Ten minutes later they were driving into the only empty parking space outside Luigi's.

'Mr Hammond!' The headwaiter, in black and red striped waistcoat and bow tie, came forward with a flourish. 'You've been a stranger . . . ' He wagged a finger, glancing with approval at Gennie. 'And you've brought a beautiful young lady to see us.'

Gennie raised an eyebrow.

Oliver coughed and glanced away to conceal his grin. 'This is Luigi,' he said.

Gennie smiled and took the extended hand. Not the headwaiter, then.

'Gennie Durham,' Oliver was saying. 'She runs the Flying Fox.'

Gennie's eyebrow arched; until that moment she hadn't thought of herself as running the pub, but now that she thought about it she realised that it was exactly what she did. It was a good feeling.

At Luigi's request she followed him

through the packed restaurant to a table by the window.

'I always save the best table in case some of my special customers come in.' He beamed up at Oliver. 'And Mr Hammond is extra special.'

Oliver was looking distinctly embarrassed as he took his seat and thanked Luigi for the menu.

As the man left, weaving his way through the tables, stopping to chat here and there with the diners, Gennie leaned across, laughing. 'Did you pay him to say all that?'

Oliver let out a sigh and then grinned. 'I promise you, I didn't. He's what you might call a welcoming host.'

'Really?' said Gennie, using the tall menu to hide her grin. 'Is the food as good as the welcome?'

'You'll have to tell me that once we've eaten.' He glanced down the list of dishes. 'I can recommend the Antipasto. It's a platter for two of buffalo mozzarella, smoked prosciutto, Milano salami, chargrilled peppers and lots of other wonderful things.'

'Sounds delicious,' Gennie said. 'I'll have the Fettuccine to follow.'

'Spaghetti for me,' Oliver said, looking up as a waiter appeared at their table.

Oliver ordered the food, and a bottle of sparkling Italian rosé wine.

'You must be so relieved about Mitch. Molly looked radiant when we left them.'

Oliver's eyes lit up. 'I don't think Dad's out of the woods yet, but yes . . . it was wonderful to see him coming round like that.' Then he frowned. 'I can't believe Will has behaved so irresponsibly. He must have known how worried we would be when he took off without a word. Heaven knows what the folks are going to make of it.' He looked up and met Gennie's eyes. 'We can't hide his disappearance for ever.'

'I'm sure we won't have to. Your brother will be back in no time. He just hasn't thought it all through.'

'You think so?' Oliver wasn't looking convinced. 'I don't like people disappearing,' he said quietly.

The wine arrived and he poured them each a glass, which they sipped in silence until their food came. The meal was every bit as delicious as Gennie had been expecting, but Oliver's mood had changed. He looked like a man with the worries of the world on his shoulders. Was he thinking about Will, or was it his business problems that had etched those deep furrows in his brow? The memory of the blonde in the car park came flitting through her mind. Was Oliver cheating on his business partner? Was that what this sudden morose mood was about? Or maybe he was just remembering that he had kissed her, and was now regretting it.

She cleared her throat. 'Look, tell me to mind my own business if you like, but I really do want to help. There's obviously something bothering you, Oliver.' She looked up and thought she caught something wary in his eyes. 'I'm guessing it's not just about Will.'

His expression darkened. 'You read minds now, too?'

His tone stung her. 'I'm sorry . . . I didn't mean . . . ' Something tightened in Gennie's throat and she looked away. Then she felt his hand covering hers.

'I'm sorry, Gennie. I know you're only trying to help, but you can't . . . not this time. There are things in my life that you know nothing about.' He gave a sardonic laugh. 'And believe me, you wouldn't want to.'

He beckoned to the waiter to bring the bill.

Gennie had been expecting the effervescent Luigi to be lying in wait for them as they left the restaurant, but he was nowhere to be seen. She was thankful, because now she just wanted to get out of there.

Neither of them spoke on the drive back to Fenwick, and Gennie wondered if Oliver would again offer to stay the night. The wine and the food were making her drowsy and she allowed her head to sink into the soft leather of the headrest. It had been a traumatic day and now exhaustion was taking over. Oliver glanced down at her and smiled.

'Tired?'

'Shattered,' she said.

He laughed. 'I know what you mean. It's been an emotional ride.' He cleared his throat. 'Gennie . . . about earlier — '

But she wasn't listening. She was sitting bolt upright, staring across the dark fields at the red glow in the sky.

'Look . . . Oliver!' She pointed. 'Over there!' Her eyes were wide with alarm. She was praying it wasn't what it looked like.

He peered out in the direction she was indicating.

'That's not the sunrise, is it? It's a fire! And it's in Fenwick!' There was rising panic in her voice now and her heart was pumping.

Oliver put his foot down and the Porsche took off at speed.

'Please don't let it be the Flying Fox,' she whispered desperately.

'Let's not get ahead of ourselves.' Oliver's voice was calm, but inside an icy tingle was beginning to hit the pit of his stomach.

5

The main street in Fenwick-cum-Marton was a scene of chaos as they drove through. Lights blazed from every home, front doors had been flung open, and all around them little groups of people stood in stunned silence.

'It's not the Fox,' Oliver said grimly. 'It's the church that's burning. It's St Stephen's.'

Gennie clamped a hand over her mouth as her eyes searched wildly for Caro and Tom. Flames leapt from every corner of the old building. Gennie counted three fire engines, and numerous firefighters, their black-streaked faces mirroring their exhaustion as they still worked frantically to save what they could of the church.

'Caro and Tom,' Gennie yelled to Oliver. 'Can you see them?' She began running towards the inferno, but Oliver tore after her, grabbing her arm.

'For God's sake, Gennie, are you trying to get yourself killed?'

Then he spotted the couple on the far side of the road. 'Look!' He pointed. 'Isn't that them, over there?'

Gennie scanned the faces, and then through the smoke, she spotted them. They had their arms around each other, staring wide-eyed, as though in a trance, into the flames.

She ran, throwing her arms around them. 'I thought . . . I thought . . . '

'We're both safe, Gennie,' Tom said, quietly, tearing his eyes away from the burning building.

'Do they know how all this happened?' Oliver was at their side.

Tom gave a hopeless shrug. 'All they've told us is that there will be a full investigation, starting in the morning.'

'Oh, Gennie,' Caro whimpered. 'They think the fire was started deliberately.'

'Deliberately? But who? Why . . . ?'

Tom shook his head wearily. 'Who knows?' he said. 'We can't take any of this in. A beautiful old building like St Stephen's destroyed in a few hours, and for what?'

Gennie saw the tears glistening in his eyes and her heart went out to both of them.

Caro began to cry softly. 'Who could

hate us enough to do this?'

'You must both stay with me tonight. I've got plenty of room at the pub,' Gennie said.

'There's no need, really. The vicarage has been spared. The fire never reached that far,' Tom said.

'Even so. I don't think you two should be on your own tonight. You've both suffered a terrible shock.'

'Gennie's right,' Oliver said gently. 'You would be much better off at the pub.' He paused, then, 'And I'll stay in my old room again tonight, if that's all right.' He looked down at Gennie and she gave him a grateful nod. She had the feeling it might be a long and harrowing night.

'What about Dandy?' Caro said bleakly. 'We can't leave him on his own in the vicarage tonight, not with all this going on. He'll be terrified.'

Gennie smiled at the thought of the couple's gangly crossbreed Red Setter. He was a lively, excitable rescue dog whom they estimated to be about two years old.

'The invitation includes Dandy. Tom and Oliver can collect him.' Gennie grinned, linking her arm through Caro's and steering her in the direction of the Flying Fox. It was gone eleven and the place was closed, but the lights were still on in the bar area, where they found Celia tidying up in readiness for the next day.

'Oh my heavens. Just look at you.' Celia came forward, arms outstretched, and folded Caro into them. 'My poor little lamb,' she said gently, stroking Caro's hair. 'What a terrible thing.'

Celia's kindness caused more tears to course down the younger woman's cheeks. Then, with a huge effort, she pulled away, swiped at her face with her hand, and sniffed. 'I'm fine, Celia. Really I am.'

Gennie handed her a tissue from her bag.

'No-one's been hurt.' She dabbed at her nose. 'And that's the main thing.'

'Thanks for locking up, Celia,' Gennie said, glancing around the bar.

'Ach, I could have done that two hours ago for all the business I've had.' She shot another sympathetic glance to Caro. 'They say the church is completely destroyed.'

Gennie winced.

But Caro just sighed. 'Well, there's not a lot of the old building left. We should know more in the morning.'

Gennie was waiting for Celia to mention the possibility of arson, but she didn't. Clearly the jungle drums had not yet started. She had no doubt that the news would have swept the village by breakfast time. She thanked Celia for staying on, and began ushering her towards the door, adding that she would probably have to call on her services again in the morning.

Celia's face dropped when she realised if she left now she would be missing out on getting the inside story about the fire, but Gennie didn't give her the chance to argue. Opening the kitchen door, she put a gentle hand on her back.

'I haven't finished cleaning up,' the woman protested.

'That's fine.' Gennie smiled. 'You've been marvellous tonight, Celia. I'll call you in the morning.'

And with that she closed the door firmly behind Celia. After giving the woman time to disappear up the hill, she slowly re-opened the door, flinching at the acrid smell of smoke that filled the whole village, and peered out along the darkened road to the activity that still surrounded the church. She was about to draw back when she saw Tom and Oliver striding towards her. They had Dandy on a lead.

'This is very good of you, Gennie,' Tom said, as she stepped aside for them to enter. 'I've told the police where to find us, but they said they wouldn't need us any more tonight.'

Caro put her arms out to him and he went to her. Dandy bounded towards them, his great plume of a tail swiping at everything he passed.

'I think we could all do with a drink,' Oliver said, stepping behind the bar without waiting for any permission from Gennie. He poured four large brandies, handing two of them to the Dents. Caro put up a hand to refuse, but Oliver insisted.

'This will do you good. Trust me.'

Caro reluctantly took the glass and sipped from it.

'I think we would all be more comfortable through in the sitting room,'

Gennie said, ushering everyone through to the back room.

'I still can't take this in,' Tom said woodenly, settling himself next to his wife on one of the sofas.

Oliver joined Gennie on the one opposite. 'Why do the police suspect arson?' he asked.

Caro answered, 'From what we can gather, the firefighters who were first into the building said they could smell petrol.'

Tom leaned forward to press his point. 'I don't keep petrol anywhere in the church,' he said.

Gennie shuddered. 'What a waste,' she thought bleakly, not realizing she had spoken the words out loud.

'We'll survive this,' Tom said, putting an arm around his wife's shoulders and giving her a squeeze.

She rewarded him with a weak smile. 'Of course we will,' she said.

Gennie could see that the couple's familiar resolve was already beginning to return and she began to relax. Getting them away from the distressing scene had been a good idea. She glanced towards the kitchen.

'Is anyone hungry? I could probably rustle up a sandwich or something.'

Caro and Tom both shook their heads.

'I'll just check on your room then,' Gennie said, getting up.

Caro caught her friend's hand as she passed. 'Please don't go to any trouble. We just need somewhere to sleep.' The brandy, and the warmth from the fire Gennie had put a light to, had Caro's eyelids beginning to droop.

'She's exhausted, poor love,' Tom said. 'Would you mind if we just go up now? We'll take Dandy with us. I'm sure the room will be fine.'

'Of course not.' Gennie moved to the door. 'I'll just show you the way.'

'They're both whacked, poor things,' Oliver said when Gennie returned a few minutes later.

She'd given Caro one of her night-dresses and found a clean pair of Will's pyjamas for Tom. She settled herself with a sigh opposite him, noticing that in her absence he had replenished their glasses.

'I'm glad you're here, Oliver,' she said quietly, not meeting his eyes.

'You all looked like you needed some moral support.'

She nodded, lifting her glass, watching the golden liquid move as she tilted it. 'I can't believe someone we know could have done this terrible thing.' She looked up at him. 'And why, Oliver? Why would anyone want to destroy a church?'

He shrugged, grim-faced. 'Who knows what damage a deranged mind might wreak.'

Gennie sat up. 'You suspect someone?' Her voice rose an octave on the last word. Then a horrible thought struck her. 'You can't be thinking Will is responsible?'

He looked at her in genuine shock. 'Will? Well, of course I don't. What made you think that?'

'Sorry. It was a ridiculous thing to say. I think my mind must have stopped working.' She hesitated and then added, 'It was just when you were taking about troubled minds — '

'I said deranged. I don't think my brother is deranged. But apart from that, none of this is Will's style.' Oliver drained the final dregs of brandy and put his glass on the low table between them.

'It's strange that we haven't heard from him, though,' Gennie said. 'I mean, I can understand him taking off in a fit of pique last night if he felt he was being made the scapegoat for the business's failings. But surely he's bound to have calmed down by now? He must know we are all worried about him.'

'Perhaps he found Saffi . . . and they've eloped.'

Gennie looked up, wondering if he was being serious. He wasn't. Their eyes met and they both laughed, releasing some of the tension built up over the evening.

'Well, maybe not,' he said at last. 'It was just a thought.'

He was still watching her as she stood up. 'If you'll excuse me, Oliver. I think I'll turn in now. I have a feeling tomorrow might be a long day.'

★   ★   ★

The four of them were having breakfast in the kitchen next morning when the police arrived. Two plain-clothes detectives followed Gennie through, eying the bacon rolls and mugs of coffee with an air of longing.

It was the older of the two who spoke. 'I'm Detective Sergeant Thornton and this is Detective Constable Eccles.'

Tom sprang up. 'You have some news for us?'

The officers exchanged a puzzled glance. The older one spoke again. 'And you are?'

Tom and Caro introduced themselves.

'Oh, I see. Last night's fire . . . it was your church. Err, no, we haven't called about that. There are other officers dealing with the arson.'

Gennie saw a shiver go through Caro at the mention of the word.

'No, it's not that. The reason we are here,' the DS continued, 'is to inquire after Will Hammond.' He looked around the room. 'This is his pub, isn't it?'

Oliver stepped forward, not bothering to correct him. 'Will is my brother. Has something happened to him?' His voice was urgent.

'We are trying to trace him, sir.' He cast another searching glance around each of their faces in turn. 'Is he here?'

93

Oliver shook his head. He had turned deathly pale.

The policeman cleared his throat. 'Perhaps we could speak in private, sir?'

'What?' Oliver said, his voice rising. 'No. Say what you have to right here, Sergeant. These are my friends.' He waved an arm to include all three of them.

'Very well. We want to interview Mr Hammond . . . about the disappearance of Sapphire Peters.'

They all stared at him in stunned silence, then Gennie said, 'Saffi hasn't disappeared. She's gone home.'

'Not according to her parents,' the officer came back. 'They think something may have happened to her.' He turned a confrontational stare on Oliver. 'And that your brother could be responsible, sir.'

Gennie was liking this pair of detectives less and less every second. She could see the anger flaring in Oliver's eyes and prayed he would keep his temper.

'That's ridiculous. If you are suggesting that my brother has in some way harmed this girl then you don't know him. He just isn't capable of such a thing.'

But Gennie was remembering the fury in Will's eyes when he flew at Oliver in a rage that night in the Hammond's bungalow. She swallowed hard. That was stupid. She was annoyed with herself for even considering such a thing. His behaviour had been totally out of character. Yet it was clear that Will had been under stress that evening. They had all assumed it was connected to the Flying Fox — but maybe not. Had there been something else worrying him? Some secret fear involving Saffi that he couldn't talk about to any of them?

'Mr Hammond is right,' Gennie said, defiance in her voice. 'I know Will, and he would never harm Saffi. He loves her.'

'Well, where is she, then?' the detective came back.

'We can't help you there. All I know is that my brother is not a criminal.'

'I think you can believe him,' Tom cut in, calmly. 'I know the two young people in question. I would suggest Miss Peters' parents are panicking. It's understandable that they should worry about their daughter, but if she is with Will Hammond then I'm sure she is perfectly safe.'

Oliver flashed him a grateful smile.

DS Thornton pressed his lips into a hard line, and then turned to face Oliver. 'I understand that your father is recovering from a heart attack?'

Gennie saw Oliver frown. How the devil did they know about that? They must already have been asking questions around the village. She shivered.

'Doesn't it strike you as odd that, under the circumstances, Will has not returned?'

Oliver bristled. 'He won't know about Dad.'

The detective let out a long and laboured sigh. 'We'll see,' he said.

The four of them stood in shocked silence after the detectives had gone. Then Oliver said, 'This is all we need. Where the hell *is* Will?'

Gennie put a hand on his arm. 'I think we need to find him . . . before the police do.'

'And just how do you propose we do that?' he returned hotly, then immediately apologised. 'I'm sorry, Gennie. I know you're just trying to help, but I'm so angry with Will for putting us in this position.'

Tom put up his hands. 'I think we all

need to take a step back here. Give your-selves time to think about things. Until now all your concerns have been for Mitch and Molly.' He paused. 'You two have been through a rough time over the past twenty-four hours. Stop worrying about everyone else. It's time to be kind to yourselves.'

Gennie felt a wave of shame wash over her. St Stephen's Church — Tom and Caro's church — had burned to the ground during the night, and here she and Oliver were, selfishly involving them in *their* problems.

Oliver must have read her mind for he stepped forward and put a hand on Tom's shoulder. 'You and Caro mustn't worry about us. My family — ' He glanced towards Gennie. ' — and that includes you, Gennie — we can look after ourselves. You, on the other hand, have an entire parish to worry about.'

His words shot through Gennie like a little dart of pleasure. Had Oliver really said that? Had he said she was one of the family?

Tom and Caro had clipped a lead on Dandy and were already heading for the door. 'We do need to get back to the vicarage. There will be many parishioners to visit today.' He gave them a wistful smile. 'Some of the older people will have been very frightened by what happened last night. We need to reassure them.'

Gennie and Oliver followed them out the back door and into the car park. Caro turned to hug each one in turn. Tom shook their hands. 'Thanks for everything,' he called back, as they turned in the direction of the ruins of St Stephen's.

'Tom's right,' Oliver said bleakly. 'We have to take a step back from this business with Will.' He was reaching into his pocket for his car keys. His Porsche was still parked opposite the church.

She caught his arm as he turned to go. 'I don't think we should tell Mitch or Molly about the police visit,' she said.

'I agree,' he said, turning to face her. His grey eyes were gentle, and for a moment she thought he was going to kiss her again. Her heart was already hammering in anticipation. But he stepped back, giving her a nod of farewell as he went to collect his car.

Five minutes later he drove into the car park. 'There are a few things needing my attention at the office, and then I'll call in to see dad.' He managed a smile. 'I'll come back this evening and keep you posted, Gennie,' he said.

She nodded and gave him a wave as he drove away.

'Give Molly and Mitch my love,' she called after him.

A hand appeared through the open car window as Oliver gave her the thumbs up. Gennie turned and slowly went back to the kitchen. She felt flat now that they had all gone. The last thing she wanted to was to spend the day preparing bar meals, yet she was sure the pub would be busy today. Tragedy and loss brought communities together — and the destruction of Fenwick-cum-Marton's only church had certainly been a loss. And since the Flying Fox was the only other community meeting place, it was more than likely that the villagers would converge here.

She rang Celia to confirm she could help in the bar, then called Jane Carter, a young local woman who was always willing to help out when the pub was busy. And she, too, confirmed that she would be available.

Gennie decided not to put full bar meals on the menu. Instead, she would offer bowls of homemade soup, served with crusty bread. Unlimited amounts of freshly-made sandwiches would also be available. She rang the baker in Sandsdyke, a small town five miles away, and placed her bread order.

By the time Celia walked in two hours later, a huge pot of lentil broth was simmering on the stove, and trays were stacked with an assortment of wrapped sandwiches.

Celia sniffed appreciatively.

'Homemade soup.' Gennie smiled. 'Gallons of it.'

'That should go down well today,' Celia said, and then paused, giving Gennie a critical stare. 'You look all in, lass. Why don't you take yourself off upstairs and have a nice relaxing soak in the bath. I can open the bar.'

She sensed Gennie was about to hug her and took a step back.

'You, Celia . . . are a lifesaver.'

Celia sniffed. 'Just happy to help out,' she said airily.

Gennie's suspicion that the Flying Fox would be busy that day had been accurate. Not only had the locals come out in force, but others had turned up from some of the surrounding villages, keen to see the extent of the fire damage to St Stephen's for themselves. Journalists from two local newspapers and a TV camera crew had also crowded into the bar. Gennie had to call in two more part-time staff to cope with the demand.

The soup ran out before one-thirty, and Gennie and one of her helpers were kept busy keeping up with the demand for sandwiches. By closing time the little workforce was ready to collapse. They gathered around the kitchen table.

'Phew,' Celia sighed, her cheeks glowing pink, 'I've worked at the Flying Fox for ten years, off and on, and I've never known it that busy.'

'Bad news always pulls a crowd,' said Janie, with wisdom beyond her twenty-odd years. She turned to Gennie. 'Can we expect the same this evening?'

Gennie was pouring boiling water into four mugs of instant coffee. 'I doubt it. Things are bound to have calmed down by tonight, but I'd like all of you to come back, if that's all right.'

They all nodded.

After they'd gone Gennie wandered around the empty tables. The bar was still ringing with the vibes of the earlier crowds. It was a strange feeling, this mix of euphoria and sadness. She felt a touch of guilt that her business had flourished today. It had been at the expense of her best friends, Tom and Caro, not to mention the missing Will and Saffi.

The good pubs were always this busy, she thought, and realised she had a hunger to repeat the performance. She walked through the restaurant, trailing a fingertip over the tables. She had a vision of the place buzzing with happy, contented diners.

The shocking events of the last two days had certainly left her both physically and emotionally drained, but there was something else beginning to stir inside her. There was a determination to give the Flying Fox a future. And she hoped she now knew how she might make that happen. If she was right, then her plan could not only help her friends, but possibly the entire community.

6

The smell of burning timbers still hung in the air as Gennie made her way to the vicarage that afternoon. Her mobile phone rang as she walked and she fished it out of her pocket, smiling when she saw Oliver's name.

'Just ringing to say Dad is still improving and wants to come home.'

Gennie laughed. 'He really must be feeling better then. That's wonderful news, Oliver.'

'Yes, I have to admit it lifted my spirits too when I saw him.' He paused. 'The trouble is that now he is feeling so much better he's asking for Will, demanding to know why he hasn't visited.'

'Oh, Oliver. What did you tell him?'

'The truth . . . well, as much of it as I could. I said he'd gone off to look for Saffi and that his phone must be out of credit or else he must have lost it. I told Dad that either way I couldn't contact him, so he didn't know he was in hospital.'

'How did that go down?'

'As you can imagine,' Oliver said, 'Dad wasn't exactly pleased.' She could hear voices in the background then Oliver said, 'Look, Gennie. I have to go. I'm in the office and a client has just walked in. I'll call round tonight about eight.'

With that he rang off, leaving Gennie to stare at the phone. She wasn't sure if she felt reassured by that call or not.

Caro was alone in the vicarage when she arrived.

'Tom's gone to York,' she said. 'The Bishop wanted to know all the details of the fire. Poor man, he's as devastated as we are. He used to be curate here, you know.' She gave Gennie a rueful grin. 'Back in the year dot.'

'I didn't realise,' Gennie sympathised. 'Will he be coming to see the damage for himself?'

'At the end of the week, I believe,' Caro said. The colour was back in her cheeks and she was beginning to look like her old self again.

'Any more news of Will?'

Gennie shook her head and repeated what Oliver had just told her. 'I'm worried, Caro. After hearing what the police had to say, it's . . . well, it's all beginning to feel a bit sinister.'

Without warning Caro sprang from her chair. 'I have chocolate cake in the fridge. It always helps.'

Gennie shook her head, laughing, as Caro disappeared into the kitchen. She would never be able to fathom out her friend's thinking. But one thing was certain. The vicar's wife was on the mend.

The Flying Fox's workforce turned up at six-thirty that evening as arranged. Gennie had already opened the bar half an hour earlier but so far only two customers had come in, neither of them familiar to her. It was so quiet she wondered if she'd made a mistake asking both Janie and Celia to work.

Bar meals would be on the menu again the next day, so she put Janie to work re-setting the dining tables, filling salt cellars, folding napkins. She'd sketched out an updated menu for the coming week, and Janie offered to type it up on the computer in the pub's tiny office and run off some copies.

Gennie was aware she had been watching the clock for the past hour. Oliver had said he'd call round at eight and it was already a quarter past. She'd left the door to the back sitting room ajar and could hear voices drifting through from the bar.

Janie popped her head round the door. 'It's getting busy out there, Gennie. I've finished the menus. Shall I go and help Celia?'

Gennie gave her a distracted nod. Oliver wasn't usually late. 'That would be great. Thanks, Janie,' she said.

She was staring into the glass of Chardonnay she'd just poured when he arrived, his big frame filling the doorway.

'Mum and Dad send their love,' he said, coming into the room and dropping onto the sofa opposite.

Gennie raised an eyebrow and Oliver shot to his feet. 'Sorry. Force of habit. I'll never get used to the fact that I don't live here any more.'

Gennie laughed and waved him back down. 'Drink?' She lifted her glass and waggled it at him.

'I'd prefer a beer, actually,' he said.

She put a finger to her mouth. 'Now let me think. Do we have any beer?'

'OK,' he laughed, getting up again. 'I'll fetch it myself.'

He returned minutes later with a pint of lager, and Gennie suspected he'd jumped the queue or had helped himself.

'That's better,' he said, settling himself on the sofa again as he wiped a foam moustache from his top lip.

Gennie lifted her own glass. 'So everything went well at the hospital?'

He nodded. 'According to Mum, the doctors are really pleased with Dad's progress. So much so that Mum feels confident enough to leave him tonight and stay at the bungalow again. I've just dropped her off there.'

Gennie's face lit up. 'That's wonderful, Oliver.'

'Yes,' he sighed, reaching for his glass again. 'One less problem.'

Gennie looked up and held his gaze.

'Things still difficult at the office?'

'Hmm . . . difficult. Now there's a word. Yes, you could say things are difficult.'

'Anything you want to talk about?' She watched his Adam's apple move as he swallowed. He returned the half-empty glass to the low table between them and wiped his mouth with the back of his hand again.

'The Fox still does the best pint I know,' he said.

Gennie sat quietly. If he was reluctant to discuss his business worries then she had no intention of prompting him again. So his next words came as a surprise.

'It's Brian,' he said. 'My business partner, Brian Wells. He's going right off the rails, and there's nothing I can do to help him.' He pressed his lips together. 'Trouble is . . . he's taking the business with him.'

Oliver's face was etched with so much worry that Gennie had to stop herself from jumping up to hug him. Then she remembered that kiss in the hospital car park again. Hadn't that been Brian's wife?

She remembered Molly's words: 'I think Oliver is having an affair with Laura.' Gennie wondered again if this could be the reason for Brian's behaviour.

She said nothing.

'He's hitting the bottle hard,' Oliver went on. 'He's not turning up for important meetings, and letting clients down. The firm can't stand much more of it.' He ran his fingers through his hair. 'Quite frankly, Gennie, I don't know what to do.'

'Do you know why he's drinking so much?' she asked, not wanting to hear the answer.

Oliver shrugged. 'Stress, I suppose. Brian is a great architect, but he doesn't handle stress well.'

Gennie swallowed. 'And do you know what is causing all this stress?

She watched Oliver's jaw tighten as he drained his glass.

'Who knows?' he said.

There was a creak from the floor above and they both looked up.

'Old timbers settling?' Gennie suggested. But she knew neither of them believed that.

Then the sound came again.

Oliver jumped up. 'Do you have an overnight guest?'

Genie flushed. 'Of course I don't.' She looked at him. 'Could it be a burglar?'

'Well there's one way to find out,' he said, striding towards the door. 'You stay here, Gennie.'

'What, and miss all the fun?' She was on her feet. 'I'm going with you.'

They crept up the stairs, Oliver holding a finger to his mouth in a 'hush' gesture. The room directly above the sitting room was Will's. When they reached it Oliver gave the door a gentle push and it swung open.

Will hadn't heard their silent approach and was rifling through the contents of a drawer.

'Welcome home, brother,' Oliver said, folding his arms and leaning his shoulder against the door jamb.

Will spun round, his eyes wide with guilt and embarrassment.

'Downstairs,' Oliver ordered. 'You have some explaining to do.'

'No!'

Gennie saw the panic in Will's face. His hair was dishevelled, his clothes filthy, and he looked as though he had been sleeping rough.

'I can't go downstairs,' he pleaded. 'Someone might see me.'

'Oh, Will, where have you been? The police have been here looking for you,' Gennie said gently.

Will grimaced. 'Saffi's parents! They threatened to call the law in.' He looked from one to the other, then said, 'They think I killed her!'

Gennie gasped and clamped a hand to her mouth.

'Oh my God, Gennie. Not you too! Of course I haven't harmed Saffi. I love her. I've been out of my mind trying to find her.'

Gennie sank down on the bed. 'I never thought you'd hurt her. I'm just shocked that Saffi's parents could think such a thing. I know how much you care for her,' she said softly.

'Saffi's folks are weird. That's why she left home in the first place, to get away from them.' He stopped. 'They have a farm in Kent from where they run this strange commune, where they all run about in white robes and have incense burning everywhere.

'People actually pay to join them. Heaven knows why, for as far as I could see, they all live in barns and sleep on straw.' His upper lip curved into a sneer of distaste. 'They've abandoned the real world — no television, no computers, no fast food — to live a life of poverty.'

He looked from Gennie to Oliver. 'Saffi didn't have a normal childhood. Are you surprised she left home?'

'Poor Saffi,' Gennie said.

'The thing is, what do we do now?' Oliver was frowning at him. 'You have to go to the police, Will, and tell them what you've just told us.'

His brother's nod was not convincing.

'But there is something even more important that you have to do first.'

Will's eyes widened in shock as his brother described their father's heart attack and how ill he had been.

'I'd no idea,' he said, his voice shaking.

Gennie stood up. 'We have to get you

downstairs and out to Oliver's car without being seen,' she said, thankful that at last she could do something.

'You can stay at the cottage tonight and I'll take you to see Dad in the morning.' Oliver's nose twitched in distaste. 'You need a shower, and to change out of those filthy clothes.'

Gennie gave them what she hoped was an encouraging smile. 'I'll go first and let you know when the coast is clear.'

Downstairs she glanced into the bar. It was noisy and packed with drinkers she didn't recognise. It would seem the St Stephen's fire was giving the village celebrity status. Janie and Celia were too busy serving thirsty customers to notice what was happening in the back room.

Gennie went back to the stairs. Oliver and Will were on the landing waiting for her signal. They looked so much like fugitives from justice that she had to stifle a giggle.

'You can come down now,' she said, going ahead of them to make sure they wouldn't be seen. She put up a hand as they crossed the kitchen heading for the back door. 'Just a minute. Let me check first.' Gennie opened the door and looked out. She saw Will's eyebrows go up when he saw the number of cars in the car park.

It seemed quiet enough. 'OK,' she whispered. 'Go now . . . quickly!'

The brothers rushed past her and into Oliver's car. Both doors slammed shut and the car took off, its tail lights disappearing out of the village towards Oliver's cottage.

She closed the door and leaned against it, closing her eyes.

'Are you all right, Gennie?' Janie said, coming into the kitchen. Seconds earlier and she would have seen Will. 'I need to change a barrel and the cellar door is locked.'

Gennie lifted down the key from its rack, her hand shaking. She forced a smile. 'Sure you can manage?'

Janie gave her a funny look. 'I have done it before, you know.'

'Yes, of course you have,' Gennie said and handed over the key.

She knew she should have gone to help the others in the bar but her legs were shaking. What she really wanted to do was to drive to Oliver's cottage to hear the rest of Will's story. He had explained that he was searching through the drawer hoping to find some clue to Saffi's whereabouts. They hadn't asked if he knew about the church. He hadn't mentioned it, yet if he'd been in the shed all the previous night, as he'd claimed, then he was bound to have known about it.

★ ★ ★

Oliver had left the porch light on so the cottage wasn't entirely in darkness when they turned into the drive. Will got out, unlocked the garage, then stood back for his brother to drive in.

'Come through,' Oliver said, unlocking the kitchen door. Neither of them had spoken during the short drive from the pub, but now Oliver wanted to know everything.

Will shook his head. 'I don't know where to start.'

'Start with Saffi. Why did she leave?'

'If I knew then I wouldn't be in this

116

mess now,' Will said defensively. 'All I knew is that I had to find her. I still do.'

Oliver had been watching him carefully. It was hard not to suspect that he was hiding something, but he decided not to push the issue, not for the moment anyway. It was more important to just let him talk.

Will took a deep breath. 'Things had been difficult between us for some time. I explained about her parents.'

Oliver nodded.

'They were always on the phone, pestering her to go home. They didn't think a pub was a suitable place for their daughter.'

'And Saffi didn't want to go home?'

'Of course she didn't.' Will looked at his brother as though he might be insane. 'They would have forced her to join that weird commune of theirs. But the fact that they were putting the pressure on her was enough to drive poor Saffi mad.'

'And that's why she left?'

'I don't know. I think so. All I know for sure is that I have to find her.' He looked up and met Oliver's stare. 'I'm sorry for flying at you like that at the folks' house. I . . . well, I suppose I just snapped. Everybody was getting at me. I know I'd let things get run down at the pub, but it wasn't my entire fault. Ask Gennie.'

He took a breath. 'All pubs are going through a bad time right now with this blessed recession. Nobody has any money. If people want a drink they buy it at the supermarket then take it home to drink.'

Oliver's brow furrowed. He knew Will was right. It was just another problem to be faced and dealt with. 'But taking off like that without telling anyone,' he protested. 'You left the Flying Fox looking like the *Mary Celeste*. Gennie and I were frantic. We didn't know what to think.'

'Sorry. That was stupid of me,' he conceded. 'I just had to get away. I'd no idea where I was going. I just drove through the night and somehow ended up at the Peters' farm. It was pointless because if Saffi had been there, her parents would not have let me see her. So I took things into my own hands. I parked up in a lane and crept about, searching for any signs that Saffi was around.

'I was spotted, of course, by some of the Peters' 'followers', as they like to call themselves.'

'Oh, Will.' Oliver's brows came down and Will threw up his hands as though in defence.

'I know, I know. It was stupid, but I was desperate.'

They were still in the kitchen, facing each other across the table. Will glanced towards the fridge.

'Got any beer?'

Oliver got up and took two bottles from inside the fridge door, and rummaged for a bottle opener in a nearby drawer. He de-capped both bottles and handed one to his brother. Will took a long pull on the beer and then smacked his lips.

'That's better. I needed that.' He resumed his story. 'I could see why the Peterses would have been suspicious of me. I mean, I must have looked like a wild man. They accused me of abducting Saffi and insisted that I had only turned up at their place because I wanted some kind of ransom.'

He looked up and saw Oliver's eyebrow arch.

'I know what you're thinking. It all sounds ridiculously far-fetched, but I'm not making it up. You don't know these people, Oliver. They're bonkers. I knew I had to get away, so I made a run for it.

'I could hear old man Peters yelling after me that they were going to call the police. Somehow I managed to make it back to my car and just took off. I kept driving until I ran out of petrol.' He winced, remembering. 'I was in the middle of nowhere with no chance of being able to find a filling station. I did the only thing I could. I abandoned the car.'

'So how did you get back to Fenwick?' Oliver asked.

'A mixture of shanks pony and kind lorry drivers who felt sorry for me. One of them dropped me just outside the village and I walked in. The place was in complete turmoil over that fire at the church. They were all too busy to notice me going past.'

He looked at Oliver. 'What happened there by the way?'

Oliver told him about the arson attack. Will stared at him in disbelief. 'The coppers think the fire was started on purpose? But that's crazy.'

Oliver nodded. 'Maybe, but it's what happened.'

'Tell me more about Dad,' Will said. 'Is he really all right now? What happened?'

He listened in stunned silence as his brother described Mitch's middle-of-the-night heart attack and the worrying hours they had all spent at the hospital. His expression was grave. 'I suppose everyone is blaming me for that.'

Oliver sighed and got up to fetch two more beers. 'It isn't all about you, Will. Just let's say, you have some bridges to build.'

It was late when Oliver telephoned Gennie. The ringing woke her and she sat up in bed, shaking the sleep from her head before she reached for it.

'Will's asleep. He's told me everything . . . well, mostly everything. I strongly suspect he is still holding something back. I just don't think now is the time to pressurise him.'

'Does Molly know he's back?' Gennie asked.

'I rang her. Couldn't stop her driving over. She said she wouldn't believe Will was back until she saw him for herself.'

'Was she angry with him?'

'At first, but frankly she was just so relieved to see him . . . ' He didn't finish the sentence, and Gennie guessed the emotion of the day was catching up with him.

'So, it's the return of the prodigal son, then,' she said drily.

'Something like that,' Oliver said, and then a thought struck him. 'I didn't wake you, did I?' He paused, embarrassed. 'I've only just realised it's after midnight.'

'No, I wasn't asleep,' she lied, pulling the duvet closer.

7

Gennie was up early next morning, determined to call on Molly before she set off to visit Mitch at the hospital.

The woman who opened the door to her was not the Molly of recent days . . . not the Molly she'd shared the long anxious hours at the hospital with. This Molly was bright-eyed, vivacious. She'd dressed her hair in a flattering way and wore a bright print dress under a pink jacket.

At Gennie's look of surprise she fingered the jacket. 'You don't think it's too bright, do you? I did wonder . . . ' Her voice died off.

Gennie shook her head. 'It's perfect,' she said. 'You look wonderful.' It was nice to have the old Molly back.

The older woman rewarded her with a delighted smile. 'You always cheer me up, my dear.' She put out a hand to draw her inside. 'But don't stand on the doorstep. Come in.'

Gennie followed her into the bungalow's bright kitchen. A sudden image of Will's eyes, full of fury, as he grappled with his brother in this very room, flashed through her mind and she shuddered. She sat down at the table, trying to erase the violent thought. That was all in the past. The Hammond brothers were together again. Old scores had been settled.

'I've just made some coffee. You'll have some, won't you?'

'Yes please,' Gennie said. 'But I don't want to hold you up. I just called in to ask you to pass on my good wishes to Mitch. I know you'll be wanting to get off to the hospital this morning.'

'It's early yet. I have plenty of time.' She passed a mug of coffee across the table and sat opposite, cupping her hands around her own drink.

Her eyes were sparkling. 'I've seen Will,' she said.

Gennie looked up, smiling. 'I'm so glad he's home again. It must be a weight off your mind.'

Molly nodded. 'Oliver is bringing him round here — ' She glanced up at the wall clock. ' — in an hour. Then we are going together to visit Mitch.' Her face broke into a delighted smile and Gennie could see what a pretty woman she still was.

Then Molly's eyes darkened. 'I just wish Oliver could sort out his business problems.'

Gennie did too. There were many questions she would have liked to ask. Was he really having an affair with his business partner's wife, for instance? But she stayed silent.

Molly Hammond was in a talkative mood. She shook her head, thinking. 'Brian is ruining his life. He drinks far too much, and he gambles.' She bit her lip. 'I just hope he doesn't drag Oliver's business down with him.'

Gennie pushed away her empty mug. 'I don't think Oliver is anybody's fool.'

'He's not, you're right. But there is a side to my son that few people ever see. And he has had some pretty heavy emotional stuff to deal with.'

Gennie arched an eyebrow. What was she talking about? What heavy emotional stuff?

Molly was talking again. 'Oliver is very soft-hearted . . . has been since he was a boy. But that sort of indulgence doesn't go well with running a successful business, so he keeps it hidden. It's one of the reasons why I know he will not turn his back on Brian. They've been friends for years. And if there is one thing I know about my son, it's that he is eternally loyal to his friends.'

Gennie frowned. This view was at odds with Molly's previous suspicions that Oliver was having an affair with Laura Wells. She was confused, and wondered why she was still giving Oliver's business so much thought. It was none of her affair. So why could she not get the image of that kiss in the car park out of her head? And what was this heavy emotional stuff Molly had talked about?

Molly was straightening up, her expression suddenly serious. 'Actually, Gennie,' she began, 'I'm glad you called round. We had intended asking you over this evening, but I can just as easily tell you now.' Her fingers fidgeted nervously with her rings. 'There's no easy way to tell you

126

this, so I'll just say it. We've thought long and hard about it.' She paused. 'We have decided to sell the Flying Fox.'

Gennie blinked. Had she heard that right? 'Sell the Fox! But you can't. I thought we had agreed to reconsider that?'

'We can't sell it . . . well, not outright, we know that. What I'm talking about is the Hammond family shares. We still own eighty per cent of the business, but with the way things are going at the moment, they will be worth nothing in a year's time. Surely you see that?'

Gennie stared at her, stunned. 'You can't sell the pub without my shares,' she protested, her voice rising.

Molly tried to smile . . . to take some of the heat out of the situation. She had seriously misjudged Gennie's reactions. 'We were rather hoping,' she began, 'now that you've had time to think about things, that you . . . well, that you would agree with us. We have a much better chance of finding a buyer if we can sell the business in its entirety.'

Gennie sat ashen-faced, unable to believe

what she was hearing. 'But you and Mitch love the Flying Fox. It's your life.'

Molly sighed. 'It was. The last few days have sharpened our minds on that. Priorities change, Gennie. At the moment the pub is just a worry. Mitch and I can see the business we loved disappearing before our eyes.' She raised her hands in a gesture of defeat. 'It breaks our hearts to do this, but we have no choice.'

She reached for Gennie's hand and gave it a sympathetic squeeze. 'I know it's hard, but it would be for the best.'

Gennie was staring unseeing at a spot on the far wall. 'And Oliver has agreed to all this?' she asked numbly.

Molly shrugged. 'I wouldn't necessarily say he's agreed, but he's a businessman, he can see the sense of it.' She looked up and found Gennie's eyes on her. 'The three of us discussed it last night. Whether we like it or not, this is the only way.'

Gennie's head was in turmoil as she walked back to the pub. Oliver would have known all about this when he called her last night, and yet he had said nothing. All this had been decided without any consideration for her views. Over the past months she had begun to feel like she was a part of this family. Now it felt as though she had just been tossed aside. The Hammonds didn't care about her. She meant nothing to Oliver!

She swiped angrily at the tears that had begun to trickle down her cheeks. She'd had plans, ideas, and a determination to make the Flying Fox thrive again. Now all hope of that was gone.

Gennie knew the only people who would consider buying the pub in its current financial state would be one of the big commercial chains. If that happened then the Flying Fox would become a mirror image of so many other, characterless venues. There would be a uniformed layout, frozen microwave food, and over-priced beer. The locals of Fenwick-cum-Marton would hate it. She was sure that losing the local business would not bother such a company. They would be after the wider market, drawing customers from a greater radius of towns and villages.

Her mind was so full of the images she dreaded that she didn't realise she had walked out beyond the village and was now surrounded by fields. Turning, she walked slowly back, letting herself into the kitchen. A car swung into the car park at speed behind her, its tyres throwing up a shower of gravel as it came to a halt. The door slammed closed, and Oliver strode towards her.

She flew at him. 'You knew . . . you knew!' she yelled. 'And you never said a word.'

Oliver put up his hands as though he expected her to strike him. 'Let me explain . . . I need to explain.'

'Too late for explanations,' Gennie fumed. 'I know now what you all think of me — and it's nothing!'

Oliver stepped into the kitchen and closed the door behind him.

'It wasn't like that.' He took her hand, but she snatched it back.

'Mum was wrong to have sprung it on you like that. She just didn't realise how upset you would be. Nothing has been decided.' He took a breath. 'Look, Gennie. Can't you understand where she is coming from? This is all about taking the stress off Dad. She's terrified of him having another heart attack.'

Gennie's shoulders slumped. 'I understand all that. But selling the Flying Fox . . . I had such plans for the place.'

'Plans?' Oliver repeated.

She tilted her chin and met his eyes. 'Yes, plans . . . improvements . . . ideas to make this place work again . . . ' Her voice trailed off. She was determined not to cry in front of him.

'You never said anything about plans.'

'I wasn't exactly given the chance,' she said defiantly. She saw his anxious glance to the clock.

'I have to go. I promised to deliver Mum and Will to the hospital and then I have to be at the office. But I'll be back. Just don't give up on us, Gennie. We'll talk. We'll find a way out of this.'

He reached across to touch her cheek and this time she did not draw away.

'I promise,' he said quietly, gazing into her eyes.

Gennie couldn't decide if she felt better or worse after Oliver's visit. 'Don't give up on us' he'd said. Had he meant the family or just him and her? She put her head in her hands. Her whole future was in turmoil. She had to think . . . to clear her mind.

What made her think she was any kind of businesswoman? She'd had this romantic idea that she could run her own village pub and had sunk all her savings into something that had been no more than a whim. Now it was all falling apart. She'd given it what she'd thought was her best efforts, and yet the Flying Fox was still losing money. Profits had slumped so low as to be almost non-existent. Her mind went back to how busy the bar had been the previous lunchtime. But that wasn't normal. It had been because of the fire. But it had brought the community together. That was the kind of spirit the old place needed now.

The vague idea she'd had that she could save the Flying Fox was taking on a new life. The plan that was seeding itself in her mind was so improbable that it just might work.

Gennie looked at the clock and frowned; it was nine-thirty already and she still hadn't made any preparations for lunch.

'You couldn't exactly call this busy,' Celia commented later, as she cast a glance over the five tables where customers were tucking into bar lunches.

'It's early yet,' Gennie conceded, but she knew the woman was right. Well, it was Thursday lunchtime. They could hardly expect to have much trade. Fridays were better, and she was already taking bookings for the weekend.

'They're still drinking, though,' Celia commented, as she pulled the first of three pints ordered by a man at the end of the bar.

Gennie went back to the kitchen to wait for her next order. At least the pub wasn't entirely devoid of customers.

Tom was not at the vicarage when Gennie called later that afternoon.

'He's at the church,' Caro said.

Gennie raised an eyebrow.

'In the ruins,' Caro explained. 'He goes there quite often. In a strange way I think he gets comfort from the place.'

'Is Tom all right, Caro?' she asked cautiously. The last thing she wanted to do was to upset her best friend's husband.

Caro nodded, but there was a glint of wetness in her eyes. 'We have good moments and bad ones,' she said. 'It's still difficult to take in what's happened.' Then she smiled and the old Caro was back. 'You should go and see him, Gennie. He'd appreciate that.'

The church, or what was left of it, was only fifty metres down the road from the vicarage, and Gennie was thoughtful as she walked. She wondered what Tom and Caro would think of the Hammonds' decision to sell the pub.

She found Tom standing in the middle of the ruins. It was a heart-breaking scene. When he spotted Gennie coming, he held out his hands to her and she took them.

'I'm so sorry, Tom.'

He sighed, his eyes travelling over the gaunt remains of the old stone walls, and the charred embers inside. 'There are practical issues to resolve. We can't dwell in the past.'

'What happens now?' she asked.

'I've arranged to hold Sunday's service

at the church in Thorndyke. It's still part of my parish.'

'But that's miles away,' she protested. 'Will your congregation be prepared to travel that far?'

'I don't honestly know. I'm hoping so. It's important that we maintain continuity. Thorndyke is not ideal, but I have no other choice.'

It came to Gennie in a flash. 'Yes, you do — and right here in the village.'

Tom gave her a quizzical look.

'You can hold your service at the Flying Fox. We have plenty of space in our function room at the back.' She grinned at him. 'That is if you don't think God will mind his flock meeting in a pub.'

Tom's face lit up. 'Miss Durham . . . I could hug you.' He took a step closer. 'In fact I think I will.' With that he threw his arms around her.

And the sounds of their laughter rang through the ruins of St Stephen's Church.

'Come with me, Gennie. There's something I want to show you.'

There was a definite spring to Tom's step as they headed back towards the vicarage. 'It's out there, in the shed. The firefighters saved it for me. They thought I would like to have it.'

He threw open the shed door and Gennie caught the smell of charred timber. The thick oak panel was propped against the back wall.

'What is it?' she asked.

Tom ran his fingers over the blackened edges of the old wood. 'It's part of the altar.'

Gennie looked at him and saw the light in his eyes.

'It will be part of the new church,' he said proudly. 'The new St Stephen's.'

Gennie's stare widened.

Tom nodded, laughing. 'That's right. It's all hush-hush, and still completely unofficial, but yes.' His grin was growing wider. 'The Bishop himself told me when I went to see him yesterday. The Diocese will finance the new build.'

'But that's wonderful, Tom.'

'It will go up right here, on the site of the old St Stephen's.'

'Like the Phoenix rising from the ashes,' Gennie murmured.

Tom swallowed. 'That's exactly how I have been seeing it.'

They walked back to the vicarage together and met Caro coming along the path with Dandy prancing around her. Gennie bent down and ruffled his soft coat.

'Why don't you join us, Gennie? You look as though you could do with a good walk across the fields.'

Gennie raised an eyebrow at Tom.

'Don't mind me,' he laughed. 'I have calls to make.'

A five-minute walk at a brisk pace took them to the end of the village, and the open countryside. Caro unlatched the gate into a field and they went through.

'Did Tom tell you our good news?'

'You mean about the church?'

Caro nodded, her eyes on Dandy, who was romping ahead. 'It's given Tom new life . . . new hope. We're very lucky.'

'It's wonderful, Caro. I'm so pleased for you,' Gennie murmured.

'I'm guessing things aren't quite so good for you at the moment,' Caro said, sliding a concerned glance at her friend. 'Want to talk about it?'

Gennie sighed, and told her about the Hammonds' shock decision to sell the pub.

'Ah, that's not good news.'

Gennie straightened and tilted her head defiantly into the wind. 'Well, it hasn't happened yet, and it won't if I have anything to do with it.'

'That's fighting talk.'

Gennie nodded. 'I'm not a quitter, Caro. And I'm certainly not giving up on the Flying Fox.' She winced, suddenly remembering something else Molly had mentioned. She turned to Caro. 'You and Tom know the Hammonds quite well, don't you?'

Caro nodded.

'Has Molly ever mentioned some terrible thing that's supposed to have happened to Oliver?'

Caro took a breath before replying, then said, 'You're talking about his girlfriend, Sophie Chandler.'

When Gennie stayed silent, she went on. 'It happened about two years ago, long before Tom and I came to St Stephen's. It's still shocking to even think about it.' She bit her lip, her hand trailing over the tall grasses as they passed. 'Poor Sophie was murdered!'

Gennie gasped, and she wheeled round to stare at Caro. 'Murdered?' she repeated incredulously.

'Her body was found under one of the bridges in York.'

'She was drowned?'

'I think she was stabbed and her body pushed into the river.' She grimaced. 'Maybe I shouldn't have said anything. I assumed you would know all about it, being so close to the Hammonds.'

Gennie felt numb. 'Did the police catch the killer?'

Caro shook her head. 'Not as far as I know.'

'You mean they're still out there?' Gennie was horrified. 'Poor Oliver. What a thing to carry around with you.'

They had completed their circuit of the large field and were now heading back to the village. Gennie's head was still reeling. Maybe she was wrong to fight the Hammonds' plan to sell the pub. They had good reason to want to leave the past behind. She pursed her lips. But Molly and Mitch had bought a bungalow in the village, and Oliver had showed no desire to leave Fenwick.

So many emotions were surging around inside her that she felt disorientated.

'Are you all right, Gennie?'

Caro's voice seemed to reach her from a long way off.

Gennie nodded, and managed a smile. 'I'm fine, just a bit shell-shocked, that's all.' She touched Caro's arm. 'But you were quite right to tell me. It helps me to understand things a bit better.'

They parted at the corner of the road leading up to the vicarage. Caro watched her friend walking away, and hoped she'd done the right thing in telling her about Sophie.

The phone was ringing in the tiny office behind the bar when Gennie let herself into the pub.

'I've been trying to contact you. Are you all right, Gennie? You haven't been answering your mobile,' Oliver said.

He thought Gennie's voice had sounded strange . . . distant. Again he felt a flurry of annoyance at his mother's misguided decision to tell her they were selling the Fox. But something else was upsetting her.

The genuine concern in Oliver's voice made Gennie's heart beat a little faster. 'I forgot to take my mobile with me when I went out. It's still lying here in the kitchen . . . sorry.'

That sounded better. Perhaps he'd imagined her distant mood? He went on. 'We're calling a family conference at the bungalow — and that includes you, Gennie. Can you come?'

She didn't have to think about it for long. There was no reason why Celia couldn't look after the bar on her own for an hour or so.

'More surprises?' she asked, unable to keep the uncertain tone from her voice.

There was silence for a second and then Oliver said, 'We deserved that. Mum had no right saying what she did to you this morning. She was getting ahead of herself, but we can discuss that later. Will you come?'

'Yes, of course I will.'

'Great. I'll pick you up about seven-thirty.'

'There's really no need to collect me, Oliver. The bungalow is only five minutes away.'

'Nevertheless, I will call for you,' he said. 'Oh, and by the way. I should mention I won't be around for most of the day tomorrow. Will ran out of petrol and abandoned his car somewhere in deepest Kent, so we're driving down to collect it.'

Gennie laughed. It was comforting to hear his voice. Her mood was already brightening at the thought of seeing him again. And from the way he was talking, she wondered if the Hammonds might be changing their minds about selling the pub.

She sighed. There was still Mitch to consider. The last thing she wanted was to be responsible for him having another heart attack. But if there were a chance of saving the Flying Fox then surely she would have to take it?

She'd also have to put up a pretty strong case, and that would mean having convincing answers to any questions the family might throw at her. In short, thought Gennie, she would have to do her homework.

As she went back into the kitchen to prepare for the evening's bar meals, a new thought crawled into her mind. Oliver's girlfriend had been murdered. Caro said it had all happened years ago, but did you ever get over something like that? She remembered Molly's words — she'd said her son had had to deal with some heavy, emotional stuff.

What could be worse than having the person you loved dying at the hands of some maniac? And why hadn't the police found Sophie's killer?

An awful thought struck her. What if it had been someone Oliver knew? Perhaps someone she knew . . . She began to feel sick. She must stop thinking like this.

The fate of Oliver's girlfriend — tragic though it was — was all in the past. The future was what was important. But what future did she have if the Hammonds went through with their plan to sell the Flying Fox?

8

Over the past few days Gennie had snatched odd moments to scan through the pub ledgers, but now she studied them in detail. She could see where some frugal savings could be made — paper towels in the loos to replace the individual cotton ones, no more free nibbles on the bar, and better use of drink promotions. But to Gennie's eyes all of these looked mean and penny-pinching, and they were hardly likely to make much difference to the profits.

She supposed they could exercise stricter control over portion sizes in the restaurant and bar meals, but Yorkshire folk had healthy appetites. She thought of the seldom-used function room. More wedding and party bookings would help.

She sat back, pushing her fingers through her hair, and then slammed the ledgers closed. The Flying Fox's income was on the slide, and Gennie could see no obvious way of changing it.

The sensible thing to do would be to ring her father. He had a small stake in the pub too, after all. Maybe he deserved a say in what was happening. But the last thing she wanted to do was to go to him with her tail between her legs and admit defeat. She'd been so sure she could do this on her own, but now ... well, it almost felt like she was drowning.

She tried to imagine what her father would do in her situation. His company, Durham Engineering, employed some forty people in Leeds. Running that wasn't anything like running a country pub, but it was still a business, except that her dad's business was thriving.

She took a deep breath and picked up the phone. 'Hi, Dad.' She tried to make her voice sound as bright as she could when he answered.

'Gennie?' Hesitation. 'Nothing wrong, love, is there?'

Gennie sighed. She hadn't fooled him for a minute. That's what made her dad such a good businessman ... he sensed things. He had a nose for trouble and met it head-on.

She gave him a resigned smile, even though he couldn't see her. 'I'm fine, Dad, honestly. How's Mum?'

'Yes, she's good. We both are. Now . . . tell me the real reason why you've phoned.'

Gennie paused before speaking. 'The thing is, Dad, I need a bit of business advice.'

'Yes?'

'I took my eye off the ball and now the Flying Fox is losing money.'

Daniel Durham listened patiently while his daughter went through the events of the past few days.

'There's no way I'm standing back and watching this pub close, Dad. I intend to fight for it. I'm just not sure how to go about it.'

There was silence while her father considered what she'd told him. Then at last he said, 'Well, for a start, Gennie, you can stop blaming yourself. It's not your fault if the Flying Fox is in trouble. This situation was probably well established long before you even moved in there.'

Gennie frowned. 'You think so?'

'Definitely. If you really want my advice I'd say you're too close to the situation at the moment, too emotionally involved in it. Take a step back. Try to see things from the pub customers' point of view. Decide what it is that they want — and then give it to them.'

She lay in bed that night mulling over what her father had said. He made it seem so simple, but he was right. She had to go back to basics. But most of all at that moment she had to stop worrying about the future of the pub. She was still trying to get her head around what Caro had told her. Someone had killed . . . murdered . . . Oliver's girlfriend, and had then dumped her body in the river.

What would her parents have to say if they knew about that, she wondered.

The wind was whistling around the old pub building. She could hear one of the shed doors flapping down in the car park, and shuddered. But she had no intentions of creeping down there to investigate.

Why hadn't Oliver told her about Sophie? The answer was obvious: he just didn't trust her enough to share his pain.

She imagined him in bed at night on his own, reliving the horror of it all. And her heart went out to him.

When she woke next morning, bright sunshine was slanting though the gap in her bedroom curtains. The storm that had raged through the night had subsided. She got up and squinted at the watery sun. 'Too bright, too early,' her grandmother would have said before forecasting bad weather to come. She wondered if Oliver and Will had set off yet on that long drive to Kent.

A feeling of gloom had settled over her last night. The pub was sliding into financial ruin and there seemed little that any of them could do about it. Her head ached and she dragged herself off for a shower.

She wasn't looking forward to the following evening's meeting. They had recently started closing on Mondays and Tuesdays. Perhaps the hours could be re-arranged to open only in the evenings mid-week. She'd heard of other village hostelries doing this. She tried to imagine the reactions of the locals if such a thing was suggested here and guessed they wouldn't be pleased. It wasn't an option she could muster much enthusiasm for either.

The main street was still deserted when she opened up later that morning. She sighed. It didn't look as though she and Celia would be rushed off their feet.

She was finishing off a tray of sandwiches for the bar when there was a light tap on the kitchen door. It opened, and Caro popped her head round it.

'Is this a bad time?'

Gennie smiled. 'It certainly isn't. Come on in. I'm in need of some cheering up.'

Caro slid a stool out from under the worktop and plonked herself down. 'Anything I can do?'

Gennie sighed and shook her head. 'Not this time, I'm afraid.' She finished wrapping the sandwiches and filled the kettle, taking two bright yellow mugs from the shelf.

'I actually came to thank you,' Caro said. 'That was a brilliant idea offering Tom the pub's function room for the service on Sunday. He's quite made up about it.'

'The Bishop doesn't mind his flock meeting in a pub then?' Gennie sent her friend a quizzical grin.

'Quite the opposite. He thought it was inspired.'

'Well, I'm glad someone's happy.'

Caro's eyes narrowed. 'There really is something wrong, isn't there? Are you brooding about what I told you yesterday about Oliver's poor girlfriend?'

'I suppose I am. I just can't stop thinking about the ordeal he must have gone through.' She looked up. 'Why didn't he tell me about it, Caro?'

'I dare say he will,' Caro said gently. 'It *was* all a long time ago. I expect he's still trying to put it behind him.'

Gennie sighed. 'It puts my small problems into perspective.' She met her friend's questioning stare and gave in. 'It's all this business about the pub. The Hammonds are thinking about selling up. It's not what any of us really wants, but the Flying Fox is losing money, and I can't see how we can improve things. I suppose I'm just finding it hard to come to terms with.'

'Surely all businesses are going through a bad patch at the moment?' Caro reasoned.

'True, but it still doesn't help us.' Gennie stretched a hand out to her friend. 'None of this affects Tom holding his service here. Well, at least I wouldn't think so.' She suddenly realised she had offered the function room without first checking with the Hammonds. Molly and Mitch were churchgoers; they wouldn't object, would they? She hoped not.

Caro's shoulders had slumped and she was shaking her head. 'The community would be devastated if the Fox closed.'

'Maybe the community should try running the pub for themselves. At least then they would see how difficult things are at the moment.'

Their heads came up at the same time and their eyes met. Caro clicked her fingers. 'That's it,' she said.

A slow smile was beginning to spread across Gennie's face. She might not be able to help Oliver, but maybe there was still some hope for the Flying Fox. 'Are you thinking what I am?' she asked.

Caro nodded, her face alight. 'The

Hammonds could sell the Flying Fox to the village. It could be a community buy-out!' She sat back, her eyes shining. 'Could it work? What do you think?'

Gennie had been mulling over a vague notion of involving the community in the running of the pub. It had seemed like a good idea at the time, but she wasn't sure how to approach such a scheme. Now her best friend was suggesting exactly the same thing. It had to be worth considering.

Caro was getting excited. 'Tom and I have been involved in one of these projects before. His last church was in a village near Halifax. The local shop was closing, so the villagers formed a co-operative to raise funds and buy the business. The community now runs it and the last I heard it was thriving.'

A little spark of hope was beginning to glow inside Gennie's chest, but she didn't want to get too eager, not just yet. 'Running a shop is a very different thing from running a pub. I can't think of a single person in Fenwick who knows anything about pub business.'

'The Hammonds do, Gennie. And so do you.'

'Wait a minute. I don't understand.'

'In a community buy-out, the group involved employs someone experienced to run the business, usually helped by a rota of volunteers.' She stopped, raising her eyebrows at Gennie. 'Well, what do you think? Would the Hammonds go for a community buy-out?'

Gennie fixed Caro with a look. 'Let me get this straight. Are you suggesting that instead of putting the Flying Fox on the market and selling up to some big leisure chain, that the family should sell to the village?'

Caro nodded. 'That's about it. The Hammonds would get their money and still be involved in running the pub, but the burden of responsibility would be lifted from their shoulders.'

Gennie smiled at her friend's enthusiasm. 'Just one small point. Even if the Hammonds agreed to this scheme, what makes you think the villagers would want to take it on?'

Caro shrugged. 'Tom always says that

every journey starts with the first step.' She looked up. 'Will you suggest it to the Hammonds?'

Gennie sat back on her stool and slowly folded her arms. 'I need to think about it,' she said.

Caro was already racing ahead of her. 'If they agree we will have to call a public meeting. I know we can count on Tom's help, and then there's Celia. She won't want to see the pub close — '

'Hang on,' Gennie laughed. 'One step at a time.'

The ringing of her mobile brought the conversation to an end. It was Oliver.

'Sorry to bother you, Gennie. But I need a huge favour.'

'Yes?'

'Will thinks he may have left the back door of the cottage slightly open when we left. Is there any chance you could drive over there to check?'

'Of course, Oliver. No problem. I'll go as soon as Celia gets here for the bar.'

'More trouble?' Caro asked as Gennie clicked her phone off.

Gennie repeated Oliver's request.

'I'll come with you,' she offered. 'I could do with a run out of the village.'

Gennie was thoughtful as they drove out of the village. Caro's community buy-out idea was spirited, but it would still mean giving up her stake in the pub. Maybe amongst all the suggestions there was a compromise?

Caro had been watching her friend's serious expression and wondered if she was thinking about Oliver. She wished she hadn't blurted out all that business about Sophie's murder. She'd regretted it as soon as she saw the look of shock on Gennie's face. She obviously had feelings for Oliver.

She glanced up. 'I didn't mean to upset you when I told you about Sophie. I'm sorry, Gennie. It just came out all wrong. Oliver obviously had nothing to do with the poor girl's murder. Searching his cottage was just a routine police procedure.'

Gennie froze. 'Are you saying Oliver was a suspect?' Her voice rose in alarm.

Oh, heavens. She was just making it worse. 'No, of course he wasn't a suspect. I didn't mean that.' Why couldn't she have held her tongue?

The blood had drained from Gennie's face. Her voice was hardly more than a whisper. 'Poor Oliver.' She could imagine the kind of gossip that must have raced around the village. No smoke without fire — isn't that what they would have been saying? How could they even think such a thing? Oliver was kind . . . compassionate. Molly had said so, but then she was his mother.

Gennie's mind drifted back to the blonde woman in the hospital car park. If Oliver was really having an affair with Laura Wells then he was capable of deceit. Maybe even worse.

A new thought was creeping into her mind, and she shuddered. She didn't even want to think about that!

It was raining when they reached the crossroads where they had to turn off for Oliver's cottage. A small red sports car travelling at speed in the opposite direction cut them off at the bend, forcing Gennie to spin the steering wheel, sending her car hurtling out of the other one's path. She braked hard, narrowly missing a ditch before the Clio came to an abrupt halt.

'Phew!' Caro said, twisting round in her seat in time to catch a glimpse of the disappearing sports car. 'That was a bit reckless. Are you OK, Gennie?'

The colour had left Gennie's face. 'I'm fine,' she said shakily. 'Did you recognise the driver?'

Caro shook her head. 'The windows were steamed up, but I've seen the car before. At least I think it was that car. Not many old red Ferraris around Fenwick.'

'You've seen that car in Fenwick?'

'Hmm,' Caro said thoughtfully. 'In the car park of the Flying Fox, actually.'

Gennie gripped the steering wheel, hoping her friend would not see she was still shaking. She had also recognised the car. She'd been thinking about it only seconds earlier. It was Laura Wells' Ferrari. But what was she doing tearing around the country lanes so near Fenwick? She had an uneasy feeling as she pulled up outside Oliver's cottage.

'I didn't know Oliver lived out here,' Caro said, giving the neat, whitewashed

157

dwelling a nod of approval.

Gennie was visualising the police team searching the place for clues to Sophie Chandler's killer.

They both got out of the car and made their way round to the back door. Gennie gave it a shove. It was locked.

'Will must have locked it after all,' Caro said. 'Better safe than sorry, though. Oliver was wise asking you to check.'

Gennie nodded. But what if the door *had* been left open? What if Laura found it that way and had gone inside? Somehow the thought of her wandering about Oliver's place when he wasn't at home sent a shiver down her spine. Her brow furrowed and she wondered if Laura Wells had even noticed she'd almost run them off the road earlier.

Her head was in a spin. She couldn't deal with all the thoughts rushing through her mind. She looked away, forcing herself to concentrate on Caro's idea for the community pub. Maybe she was right and it was exactly what the village needed, but Gennie wasn't comfortable about handing the Flying Fox over for the village to run. That was her job.

That evening she cleared a space on the desk in the pub's office. She'd gone over the ledgers before, but now she studied them in microscopic detail. On the face of the figures before her the Flying Fox probably wasn't viable any more. Unless . . .

She began tapping into her laptop, poring over new websites, printing out information from others. By the time she sat back, rubbing her eyes and stretching, it was well past midnight. She'd spend more time in the morning presenting her business plan in a professional way. Would it be enough to change Mitch and Molly's mind about selling the Fox? She still wasn't sure, but she had everything crossed.

It felt like the middle of the night when Gennie's mobile began to trill on her bedside table. She reached out sleepily. The clock on the tiny illuminated screen showed it was just before six. It was Will. She frowned.

'What's up, Will? Do you know what time it is?'

'Something terrible's happened, Gennie!' he blurted out. 'I think you should get over here.'

She shot up in bed, fully awake now. Fear was gripping at her heart. 'What's happened, Will?'

'It's Oliver!' She could hear the panic in his voice. 'The police have arrested him.'

'What!' She stared at the phone. 'Look, Will, just try to calm down and tell me what's happened.'

She could hear him clearing his throat. 'The police came with a search warrant about an hour ago and turned the place upside down.' He paused, gulping. 'Oh, God, Gennie . . . they think Oliver murdered Sophie!'

It took her less than fifteen minutes to get to the cottage. Will met her at the door and followed her back inside. She glanced around, shocked at the untidy mess the police searchers had left.

She reached for his hand. 'Try to stay calm Will, and tell me what happened.'

Will took a breath. 'We were wakened by this thumping on the door. Oliver got up and went to see what all the ruckus was about.' He hesitated. 'It was the police . . . and they had a warrant to search the cottage.'

Gennie stared at him. 'But why have the police arrested Oliver? He had nothing to do with Sophie's murder.'

There was a look of disbelief in Will's eyes. 'They took a long-bladed knife from the cutlery drawer. I think it was the one Oliver used to cut fruit. Anyway, they took it away in one of those evidence bags.'

Gennie froze. She was picturing Oliver slicing wedges of lemon for her drink when he'd invited her into the cottage a few days earlier. Everyone had knives. They couldn't have arrested him for that.

'They found something else upstairs. I didn't see what it was, but the police got pretty excited about it.'

Gennie's mind was working. She glanced at her watch. It was almost seven. 'Does Oliver have a solicitor?' she asked.

Will nodded. 'Simon Thirwell. He'll be in Oliver's contacts book, but the police took that as well.'

Gennie was already flicking through the phone book. The solicitor's answerphone gave a mobile contact number and she quickly punched in the numbers, handing her phone to Will when Thirwell answered.

She listened as Will went through the morning's event, nodding into the phone.

'He's on his way to the police station,' he said, handing the phone back.

Gennie's first instinct was to hurry down there to support Oliver, but she guessed it would be at least an hour before Simon Thirwell managed to see him and discover enough to tell them what was happening. She'd use the time to get back to the Flying Fox, shower and change, and ring Caro to explain the situation. It would be good to have her on standby in case she needed to call on her help later.

An hour later she and Will were on their way to the police headquarters in York. They had only been in the waiting room for a few minutes when Simon Thirwell appeared.

'The police took a knife from Oliver's cottage. It's similar to one they believe was used to kill Sophie.' He stopped, a worried expression in his eyes. 'They've also got a letter.'

'Letter?' Will and Gennie repeated in unison.

'It was hidden in a drawer in Oliver's

bedroom. It's from Sophie.' He produced a folded sheet from his briefcase. 'I'm not supposed to have this, but let's just say I have a contact here. It's a copy of the original.'

He handed it to Will. Gennie read it over his shoulder.

Sweetheart,
I think our little fling has run its course. We both knew it wouldn't last, not when I'm still in love with you know who.
It was fun, so don't be sad. Don't think too badly of me.
Sophie x

Gennie looked at it. 'This isn't proof of anything. There's no date . . . and it doesn't even mention Oliver.'

'Exactly,' the solicitor said. 'And Oliver says he's never seen it before.'

'So how did it get into Oliver's bedroom?' Will asked. 'And why now? It's two years since Sophie was killed.'

A worrying suspicion was creeping into Gennie's head. Oliver thought Laura was stalking him. And she and Caro had seen her car near his cottage that day. She thought of the elegant woman in the hospital car park and dismissed the idea. She couldn't quite see Laura Wells brandishing a knife. If she was going to kill someone, poison would probably be more her style.

'I agree.' Thirwell nodded to Will. 'We should know more later today when the handwriting has been checked and the note scanned for fingerprints.'

'Why did the police suddenly decide to search Oliver's cottage?' Gennie asked.

'They had an anonymous tip-off.'

Gennie's expression was grim. 'From the person who set him up, obviously.'

Thirwell nodded. 'It would seem so. But look, there really is no point in both of you stopping here. You won't be allowed to see Oliver. I'll ring as soon as there is any more news.'

'Simon's right,' Will said, turning to Gennie. 'You'll be needed back at the pub. I'll hang on here, anyway.'

'What about Molly?' Gennie asked. 'She needs to know about this.'

Will nodded. 'I know,' he said solemnly.

'I've been putting it off.'

'Would you like me to tell her?' Gennie offered. 'I could call in at the bungalow on my way back.'

Will's eyes lit up. 'Would you?'

Molly Hammond was outraged when she heard the news of her son's arrest.

'Oliver had nothing to do with that girl's murder. What do the police think they're playing at?' she raged.

'Will is still down there, and Simon Thirwell has promised to ring as soon as there is any news. I think he expects him to be released later.' She wasn't at all sure this was the case, but she was keeping her fingers crossed.

As things happened, she was right. The call from Will came early that afternoon. 'Released without charge,' he announced triumphantly. 'Oliver wants me to bring him straight to the pub.'

Gennie's heart contracted at the first sight of Oliver. He was unshaven, wearing jeans and an old sweater, and his eyes were angry.

Gennie put her arms around him. 'Thank God,' she whispered. 'That must have been an ordeal.'

He shook his head and sank onto the sofa. 'Somebody out there doesn't like me, Gennie.'

She sat down beside him. 'Mr Thirwell says it was an anonymous tip-off. Do you know anyone sick enough to do such a thing?'

He shrugged. 'They found a letter in Sophie's handwriting taped under a drawer in my bedroom. I've no idea how it got there, but Thirwell read me a transcript.' He swallowed. 'Sophie may have written it . . . but it certainly wasn't to me.'

She felt him shudder as she put an arm around him and knew he was re-living the horror of Sophie's terrible death all over again.

'I know this can't be easy, Oliver,' Gennie said quietly, 'but you have to try to put this terrible business behind you. The police will get to the bottom of it.'

He gave her a bleak look. 'You're right, of course. It's out of my hands now.'

9

They decided to walk up to Molly and Mitch's bungalow that evening. Gennie was wary of curious looks from the locals, but those they met just nodded their usual greetings. She began to relax. One of the benefits of living in an isolated cottage meant it took longer for gossip to spread. But she had no doubt that Oliver's arrest — no matter how innocent — would soon be common knowledge.

He'd been quiet on the short walk and Gennie sensed he was still in shock from the day's events. She hadn't noticed him glancing down at her and started when he spoke.

'You mustn't worry about this meeting tonight,' he said, reaching for her hand.

Right now, she didn't care what happened to the Flying Fox. All that mattered was Oliver. He hadn't deserved the way the police had treated him. It wasn't his fault that his girlfriend was murdered. Hadn't he been through enough?

She forced a bright smile, but inside her stomach was churning. Someone had set Oliver up . . . had wanted him charged with murder when he was completely innocent — and that someone had planted Sophie's letter. It had to be Laura Wells!

Molly and Will were waiting for them. A log fire crackled in the grate and table lamps cast a cosy glow around the small sitting room.

'Oliver!' Molly rushed forward as they came in and threw her arms around her son. 'Are you all right?' Her worried eyes searched his face. 'Come and sit down. Tell us what happened.'

Oliver gave a resigned smile and then related the day's events.

Molly's fingertips went to her temples as she stared disbelievingly at him. 'How could the police even *think* you had anything to do with Sophie's death?'

'Well they don't,' Oliver said. 'Not any more. So you can stop worrying, Mum.'

'It's pretty obvious that note was planted in Oliver's room to throw suspicion on him,' Will cut in.

'But why?' Molly's brow furrowed. 'Who would do such a horrible thing?'

The others exchanged a look, and then Oliver cleared his throat. 'It's all in the past now.' He glanced at Gennie. 'I think we should all try to put it behind us.'

Molly nodded slowly, but from the look in her eyes, Gennie guessed it would be quite some time before she could forget that her son had been arrested for murder.

Oliver had put the ledgers he had been carrying for Gennie on the low coffee table, and was nodding towards them. 'I think we have some business to discuss.'

Molly glanced down at them, and her eyes narrowed. 'What? Oh, yes.' She turned to Will. 'Pour a drink for Gennie and Oliver, dear,' she said.

Will raised an eyebrow at Gennie.

'A small sherry, please,' she said.

'Whisky for you, Oliver?'

Oliver nodded, moving to sit next to Gennie on the sofa opposite his mother.

'Well now, my dear.' Molly straightened. She was back in business mode. 'Did you manage to take a look at our books?'

'Well, actually — ' Gennie started.

But Molly interrupted. 'Will and Oliver have been chastising me for speaking too hastily.' She paused. 'What do you think, Gennie? Was I too hasty, or do you agree that we have no option but to sell the pub?'

Gennie took a deep breath. 'I actually have a few suggestions to make there.' She saw them exchange looks, and reached into her bag to draw out the sheaf of papers she'd brought with her. 'I've been doing some figures of my own and have come up with a business plan.' Out of the corner of her eye she could see Oliver's eyebrow arch and hoped it was a good sign.

She swallowed. 'As Molly says, on the face of it things don't look good, but it's no wonder we are losing money when the pub is shut half the time.'

Molly's chin came up and her back stiffened. 'There's no point in opening the pub when we don't have any customers. That's just throwing money away.'

'But isn't that just the chicken-and-egg situation? People have got used to the bar being closed on Mondays and Tuesdays, so they don't come. What if we give them a reason to come back?' She had everyone's attention now. 'I believe we should be open *every* day. We can restrict the hours, opening just from noon until three, and then again from six until eleven. And we can serve food so good that the reputation of the Flying Fox as an eating place will be known all over Yorkshire, and beyond.'

Molly wasn't looking convinced. 'It's all very well having aspirations to offer the best pub food in the county, but have you worked out how we could afford a chef of that calibre?'

'We don't have to,' Gennie said. 'We offer the concession of our kitchen facilities, for which the successful candidate would pay. In turn, he or she would basically run his or her own business, albeit from our premises.

'The chef would pay for all supplies and ingredients . . . and take all the profits.' She paused, searching each face in turn, trying to gauge a reaction. Only Oliver was smiling.

'It's a very clever idea.' He turned to Molly. 'What do you think, Mum?'

171

Molly's brow creased. 'You mean we don't get any profits from the food? But that doesn't make sense.'

'We don't directly profit from the meals,' Gennie agreed, 'but the bar would get the extra revenue, and since most people have a drink before their meal and wine with their food . . . ' She let the sentence die away, hoping her words were sinking in.

Will crossed the room and eased himself into a chair. 'Sounds like a pretty fail-safe idea to me.' He shrugged. 'I don't see how we can lose.'

'But opening the pub every day,' Molly started. 'How can we justify that if we don't have any customers?'

'I've thought of that,' Gennie chipped in. 'Granted, we might have to make a leap of faith, but I had an idea there too. We could actually open the bar a bit earlier — that's what I meant about flexible times — and run it as a kind of coffee shop, somewhere the mums and babies, the housewives, and the older village residents could meet up for a drink and a chat.

'To be really sure of getting the customers, we could offer a free scone with every drink.' She saw Molly's brows knit. 'It does actually work. I know a hotel that does this very thing and it has a crowded bar every morning.'

Oliver leaned towards her, forcing her to look at him. 'You've really thought this out, haven't you?' There was an unmistakable glint of admiration in his eyes. It gave her the courage to continue.

'The Flying Fox needs to become a community pub again, the kind of pub that makes the locals regard it as their own. We could re-start the darts nights, the pool league, buy some bar games, and provide morning newspapers. None of these things cost much money, but they all attract customers. And then there's the function room — '

Molly put a hand up, laughing. 'Slow down, Gennie. I'm still trying to take all this in. No one could fault your enthusiasm, but we come back to the same issue all the time. The Flying Fox just isn't making money any more.'

'That's why I've made some costings,'

Gennie said, handing round the printed sheets. 'It's all detailed there.'

She waited, holding her breath while they scanned the figures. Then Oliver looked up and said, 'Good work, Gennie. You've done a damned good job putting all this stuff together.'

'You have indeed,' Molly agreed, her eyes still on the sheet. 'But these figures show us making a profit.'

'Exactly,' Gennie enthused. 'I've detailed the likely costs for the changes, plus the projected profits we could expect if the business was properly managed.' She took a breath. 'And that's the next part of my proposal — a manager.'

Molly frowned. 'But isn't that what you and Will are already doing, dear?'

'What we're doing is keeping an eye on things.' She gave Molly her most endearing smile. 'What I'm suggesting — ' She gave a little cough. ' — requesting . . . is that you make my position official. I'm not only asking you to reconsider selling the pub, but to make me manager, with responsibility for running the place and the authority to make decisions.'

She looked at Will and he nodded enthusiastically. Then she glanced at the other two. 'Give me the chance to turn the Flying Fox around. I know I can do it,' she pleaded.

There was silence in the room, and then Molly said, 'You mentioned the function room. That's always been a bit of a white elephant. I mean, it's not as if we actually get many functions.'

Gennie was remembering she hadn't asked Molly's permission before offering Tom the use of the room for his services. 'I have a confession to make. I told the vicar he could hold his Sunday service there.' She cringed. 'I know I should have checked with you first, but it just kind of happened.'

But Molly was smiling. 'It's exactly what Mitch and I would have done.'

'You mean you're not annoyed with me?'

Molly shook her head.

'I'm so glad.' She hadn't touched her sherry and reached for it now, taking a substantial sip that half-emptied the tiny glass. 'But you're right about the function room. We will need a plan for that as well.'

She was feeling euphoric. They'd listened to all her suggestions and, although Molly had voiced a few reservations, nothing had been ruled out. It had gone better than she'd dared to hope. She stood up. 'I should be getting back. I don't like leaving Celia to run the bar on her own for too long.'

'You're taking on a lot, you know,' Oliver said, on the way back to the pub.

Gennie shot him a look. 'Are you suggesting I'm not up to it?'

'Hey . . . ' He grinned, putting an arm round her shoulders and giving her a squeeze. 'Don't get your hackles up. It's you I'm thinking about.'

They'd reached the pub. Neither of them missed the fact that, apart from Oliver's sports car, there were only three other vehicles in the car park.

'Well, I think it could work. Don't you?' She stopped to look up at him.

Oliver pursed his lips. 'Let's just say it has possibilities.'

'That's a bit non-committal.'

'The decision ultimately lies with Mum and Dad. Will and I are obviously in favour of your suggestions. Personally I think you've come up with some real winners, but more importantly, you're so passionate about it, and that means everything.'

'You could put in a good word for me with your parents.' She smiled up at him hopefully, and saw him swallow.

'That goes without saying.' He cleared his throat. 'Look, Gennie. I don't think you should be here on your own at night, not when there's an arsonist still on the loose. It's just not safe.'

Gennie stared at him, wondering if he considered she was also in danger from whoever was trying to frame him. 'Are you suggesting that I hire a bodyguard?'

'I'm suggesting you agree to my moving into my old room for the time being.' He paused. 'At least until the police have arrested someone for the church fire.'

The thought of Oliver sleeping under the same roof as herself had already started her heart thumping.

'I'll take your silence for acceptance then,' he said briskly. 'I just need to collect a few things from the cottage and I'll be back within the hour.'

'Hang on, Oliver. I haven't agreed to anything yet. And besides, what would people say? They'd think that we — '

'Let them,' he said, a mischievous glint in his eyes.

Gennie had never actually considered herself at risk here on her own at nights, but after the fire in the church . . . well, if there was a madman going about setting fire to buildings, then she would feel safer knowing Oliver was in the next room. The police may have considered him capable of murder, but they didn't know him like she did. She smiled. She had nothing to fear from Oliver.

'I hadn't considered the dangers,' she said, 'but you're probably right. Maybe it would be sensible for you to move in for a few days.' She looked up and met his eyes in the darkness. 'Thanks for offering.'

He gave her a strange look and opened his mouth to speak, and then thought better of it.

There were more customers in the bar than Gennie had expected, but Celia seemed to have everything well under control.

'How did the meeting go?' she asked.

Gennie nodded. 'Quite well, I think. How have things been here? The bar's not as quiet as I'd expected.'

'It's the fire,' Celia explained. 'It's still bringing out the curious.'

Gennie looked round the bar. Four of the tables were occupied and there were at least six people standing chatting around the bar itself. She only recognised four faces. The others were all strangers. News of Oliver's 'invitation' to the police station still didn't seem to have reached the village.

'You can get off now, Celia, if you want.' She nodded to the clock. 'There's only another half hour to go before closing time.'

'I don't mind staying on.'

Gennie put her arm around Celia's shoulder, guiding her towards the door. 'You've done enough hard work for one night. Go home and put your feet up. I'll finish off here.'

'Well, if you're sure.'

Gennie smiled. The barmaid had needed no real persuasion. Her coat was on and she had left the pub in less than a minute. It was best that Celia shouldn't see Oliver's car arrive after closing time.

Gennie had just waved off the last of her customers and locked the pub's heavy oak door when he turned up. She went through to the kitchen to let him in, feeling oddly embarrassed at the sight of his overnight bag.

'I was just about to make some hot chocolate. Will you join me?'

'Something stronger for me,' he said. 'I could be persuaded by a glass of Glenmorangie.'

'No problem,' Gennie laughed. 'I'll pour you a double while you take your things upstairs.'

He was back five minutes later. Gennie had left his glass of single malt on the small table by the side of one of the sofas and was emerging from the kitchen, her mug of steaming hot chocolate on a tray with some savoury biscuits.

'Stressful day?' he asked, watching her push her fingers through her short blonde bob.

'Not as bad as yours.' She bit her lip. 'What's Will saying about you spending the night here?'

'He's looking forward to having the cottage to himself. He's still brooding about his girlfriend going off like that.'

'Has he been to the police? I didn't like to ask earlier.'

Oliver nodded. 'Yes. They didn't really believe he had anything to do with Saffi's disappearance. He wouldn't have gone looking for her at her parents' house if he'd harmed her. It's really Saffi they want to track down.'

He repeated the story Will had told him the night he'd got back. 'He says Saffi's parents run some kind of hippy commune down there in wildest Kent. Apparently they were trying to force her to join them, which is why she left home.' He shrugged. 'I would have thought a hippy commune would have been right up her street.'

'Oliver!' Gennie laughed. 'If you mean because of the Goth thing, you've got the wrong end of the stick. Quite the contrary, actually. I think all the odd flowing clothes and black eye make-up was just Saffi's way of rebelling. Oh, she enjoyed flaunting the image, but she is no more a Goth than you or I.'

Oliver raised an eyebrow. 'I didn't know you were so well informed.'

'I'm not. I've just had more conversations with her than you have. She's let her defences slip a few times, so I know she wasn't happy.'

'Still doesn't explain why she dresses up like that. Will doesn't do it.'

Gennie wrinkled her nose. 'It's a cult thing, isn't it? If anything, I think Saffi is more punk than Goth — all those rings and leather, the long teased-out auburn hair. It's all about making a statement. Underneath all that stuff is a very vulnerable young girl.'

'I'm not sure I buy that, but like you say, Gennie, you know the girl better than I do. Her attitude didn't exactly endear her to the village. People think she looks down her nose at them.'

'Any minute now you'll be saying you don't know what Will sees in her.'

Olive raised his shoulders and lifted his glass again.

'Don't be too quick to judge. People fall in love for the strangest of reasons. And there is no doubt that your brother loves Saffi.' Gennie's voice had suddenly grown quiet. She was aware that he was studying her. The image of Laura Wells kissing him in the hospital car park suddenly flew into her mind. She reached for her hot drink, but he caught her hand and raised it to his lips.

'I'm very fond of you, Gennie,' he said gently.

Her heart was pulsing. She wanted to go into his arms, feel his lips on hers, but something held her.

She drew her hand away, wrapping her fingers around the hot mug.

'Was everything all right when you and Will got back to the cottage last night?' It was an effort keeping her voice calm.

'All right?' he asked, frowning. 'Why shouldn't it have been?' He'd gone back to his whisky, glaring into the glass like he wanted to smash it in the fireplace.

'Will leaving the cottage door open like that, I mean.'

She'd got his attention now. 'But you said he hadn't. You said the back door was locked.'

She had no idea why she hadn't

183

mentioned seeing Laura Wells' Ferrari that day. She moistened her lips, avoiding his eyes. 'It was locked . . . but I just wondered . . . ' The words died away.

Oliver was giving her a curious look. 'Wondered what?'

Gennie hesitated. 'Caro was with me and . . . well, we were almost run off the road by some maniac in a speeding car. It came from the direction of your cottage.'

She saw the muscle in his jaw working. 'Did you recognise the driver?'

Gennie shook her head. 'It was raining. The windows were steamed up,' she said cautiously. 'I think it was . . . a Ferrari.'

She hardly dared look at him, but when she did his face was ashen. 'Do you know anyone who drives a car like that, Oliver?' Her voice was barely above a whisper.

He was staring unseeing into the remains of his whisky. 'I do as it happens,' he said flatly.

Gennie held her breath.

'Brian, my business partner . . . his wife, Laura, drives a Ferrari.'

Was it her imagination, or was Oliver's voice shaking?

'Perhaps she came to see you and found the back door open,' she started. 'And when she realised you weren't at home, she closed the door and drove off again.'

They stared at each other for long seconds, the unspoken implication suspended in the silence between them. Then Oliver, his voice icy cold, said, 'You think Laura planted Sophie's note.' He was staring at her from under lowered brows.

'I don't know what I think.' She gave a nervous cough. 'You know her, Oliver. Is she capable of doing that?'

He was on his feet, striding around the room. 'Never! Laura would never do such a thing.'

But, clearly, he was considering the possibility.

'Sophie was a very beautiful woman, but she liked to play games. She manipulated people. She could have written that note to anyone.' He grimaced. 'Maybe even to the person who killed her.' He swung round, and Gennie caught the look of suspicion in his eyes. 'So you see, there

185

is no way Laura could ever have had that note.'

He stared into her face, perhaps seeking courage for what he needed to say next.

Suddenly Gennie didn't want to know. She didn't want to hear his confession that he was having an affair with Laura Wells.

She was on her feet. 'It's been a long day, Oliver. I need to get some sleep.'

He blinked, a look of confusion briefly flitting across his face, and then he drained his glass. 'I'm going to have another one of these before I turn in,' he said stonily. 'I'll make sure everything is secure.'

She lay in the darkness listening for him. It was half an hour before she heard his footsteps on the landing, then the click of his bedroom door. When it was all quiet, Gennie closed her eyes and went to sleep.

10

It had rained again during the night and the road out of Fenwick-cum-Marton still glistened wet as Gennie pulled her coat tighter against the early morning chill. The untidy scatter of twigs and branches on the paths was evidence that autumn had arrived. She'd crept out before Oliver was awake, glancing at the dark blue Porsche as she'd passed it in the car park. It would be all over the village before breakfast that Oliver had spent the night. The fact that most people would assume that they had spent the night 'together' was neither here nor there.

Early morning walks were not a normal part of Gennie's fitness routine. She preferred to take her exercise in the afternoons when most of the day's work was already under her belt. But this morning she just had to get out of the pub. The place had suddenly felt claustrophobic and she longed to be outdoors feeling the wind tugging at her hair, and the sharp breeze stinging her face.

She picked up pace as she left the village, but her thoughts still drifted back to the pub — and Oliver. The previous night's conversation had left her even more confused than she'd been before. Was Oliver actually having an affair with his business partner's wife? If he wasn't, then why was he defending her so forcefully?

Someone had planted that false evidence in his cottage. If it wasn't Laura, then who? She tried to imagine who would have access to Oliver's place. There was Will, of course, and his parents, although she wasn't sure any of them would have keys. But if they did then perhaps someone they all knew had managed to steal and copy them. Or, then again, maybe she'd just read too many detective novels.

She forced her thoughts away from the situation and tried to imagine her embarrassment if she'd wandered out of her room in her nightie and met Oliver at the bathroom door. She wondered what he would think when he did get up and realise she had gone. Would he be worried?

No, why would he? Lots of people took early-morning walks. He wasn't to know that Gennie wasn't one of them.

Out across the fields she could see a figure walking with a dog. An arm came up and waved at her. She peered at the shape, trying to make out who would be up and about at this time of day. Then she knew, and a smile split her face. It was Caro and Dandy. She waved both arms back at them and began to run across the fields. The Red Setter came from the opposite direction and they clashed in a rush of doggy excitement, all legs and flying ears.

'Put her down, Dandy,' Caro cupped her hands and shouted from the distance. 'You don't know where she's been.'

They were laughing as they met, breathless, in the middle of the wet field. 'What on earth are you doing wandering about at this time in the morning?' Caro's eyes narrowed.

'Have you no control over your dog?' Gennie joked, avoiding the question.

'Down, Dandy!' Caro pointed to the ground, but the dog ignored her. 'I'm still training him,' she said, trying to keep a straight face.

They linked arms and walked on together. 'So, what are you doing out here? Couldn't you sleep?'

'I just felt like a walk.' Gennie gave her friend a sideways glance. 'Doesn't have to mean there's anything wrong.'

Caro was studying her profile as they walked. 'But there is something . . . I can tell.'

Gennie pressed her lips together. She had picked up a branch and now hurled it into the distance. Dandy bounded after it. 'Oliver stayed the night.'

Caro's eyes widened.

Gennie whacked her arm, laughing. 'Not like that! He was worried about me being on my own in the pub, with the arsonist still at large, I mean.'

Caro's eyes darkened and she glanced back towards the village. 'I never thought of that . . . not that he would do it again. But I can understand why some people might be nervous, especially those living on their own.' She turned to stare at Gennie. 'You don't really think he will strike again, do you?'

'Of course I don't. Oliver is just being a bit over-cautious. It's his nature. He insisted on staying overnight.' She sighed. 'The village gossips will have a field day.'

Caro giggled. 'I don't imagine anyone will be scandalized.'

What would cause scandal would be the news of Oliver's arrest the previous day. It was bound to get out and Caro would wonder why she hadn't mentioned it. But she couldn't go over the whole business again . . . not yet. Her friend would understand.

They walked on, taking turns to throw the branch, which Dandy kept retrieving.

'I've been doing some hard thinking about the future of the Flying Fox,' Gennie said.

'You mean my community buy-out suggestion?'

'Well . . . partly. I think the community pub idea is a great one,' she faltered. 'But only if we can keep it in the family.'

'You've lost me,' Caro said.

'Well, I hope you don't mind, but I pinched some of your ideas. I suggested to Molly that we should run our own community-style pub.' She gave Caro a detailed account of her presentation to the Hammond family.

'Wow! You don't let the grass grow. What brilliant ideas. What did Molly say? Was she in favour of your plan?'

Gennie shrugged. 'Maybe . . . it's hard to tell. Oliver and Will were all for it, but everything depends on what Mitch says.' She glanced at her watch and pulled a face. 'I should get back. I've promised a certain vicar the use of our function room this morning, and if it's not ready in time for his service he might never speak to me again.'

'Need any help with that?' Caro grinned.

'I never refuse an offer of help.'

'Consider it done, then. Tom and I will be there in an hour or so.'

They had reached the road and turned left towards the village.

'I saw your friend again, by the way,' Caro commented, as they passed the first cottages.

Gennie raised an eyebrow.

'You know . . . the flash red sports car.'

Her eyes narrowed. 'I didn't get a really good look at the driver, but I know I've seen the car before. Maybe they live around here.'

An icy shiver had shot through Gennie. 'Where did you see the car again?' She was struggling to keep her tone casual.

'Driving past the pub. Tom usually takes Dandy for his last walk of the day, but he was busy on his sermon, so I offered. It was dark, but I'm certain it was the same car. And I think it was a woman driving.'

Had Laura been checking up on Oliver? Had she seen his car in the pub car park? Gennie realised she was shaking. Should she tell him?

The appetising smell of grilled bacon and fresh coffee greeted her as she walked into the kitchen. Oliver, in jeans and black tee shirt, looked up and grinned. 'I hope you're hungry. I've cooked the best part of a hog roast here.'

Gennie smacked her lips. 'I could do a lot of damage to a bacon sandwich.'

'Just what I was hoping to hear you say. Sit down.'

He had put rolls in the microwave to warm

through and was now splitting them and spreading them with creamy yellow butter.

'You didn't have to do all this.' She smiled, taking in the set table, the jug of orange juice and pot of percolated coffee. He had even taken a few flowers from the vase on the windowsill and cut them to posy size to make a centrepiece.

Gennie slipped off her coat and went to wash her hands in the sink, then slid gratefully onto one of the kitchen stools. The awkwardness of the previous night had vanished. They were completely at ease with each other again. Would all that change if she told him now about Laura?

'I can give you a hand setting up the function room for Tom's service this morning if you like,' he offered when she told him she'd have some cleaning up to do.

Gennie swallowed her mouthful of bacon roll and dabbed a trickle of butter from the corner of her mouth. 'Thanks, Oliver. I'll take you up on that.' There was no point in mentioning that Tom and Caro had also offered.

It had been some weeks since the

Flying Fox had hosted a function and Gennie realised with dismay that she should have arranged for the room to be cleaned before today. What had she been thinking of, not attending to this sooner? She stood in the middle of the large room, frowning at the dusty floor. The tables and chairs, stacked neatly at the far end would also need a good clean, she guessed. She put her hands to her head. 'I should have organised all this ages ago. We'll never have it ready in time.'

Oliver came up behind her and touched her shoulder. 'I'll get the brushes and you fetch the basin,' he said. 'We'll have this ready in no time.'

Gennie stared at him. The thought of the refined Oliver, with his elegant business suits and pink silk ties, sweeping the floors of the Flying Fox made her blink. Then she remembered how pristine and neat his cottage was. And besides, he wasn't in his suit today; his jeans and tee shirt were casual. She realised he was looking at her, waiting for instructions.

'This is really very good of you, Oliver.' She flushed, pointing him in the direction of the broom cupboard.

They were halfway through sweeping the floor when Caro and Tom arrived. They took off their jackets and, without instruction, picked up the other two brushes and began sweeping. Half an hour later the function room was done and dusted and the four of them had begun to set out the chairs in semi-circles around the table Tom had placed to represent the altar.

Gennie ran to fetch the vase of yellow and white chrysanthemums from the kitchen and placed them on the makeshift altar. When they had finished they all stood back surveying their work.

'Well, Tom. Will it do?' Gennie asked, catching her bottom lip in her top teeth as she cast a critical eye over the room.

'It's perfect,' he said, turning to smile at her, his arm around his wife's shoulder. 'We just couldn't be more grateful.'

Celia was amongst the first of the congregation to arrive less than half an hour later. She glanced along the rows of chairs. 'Very impressive,' she said, nodding her approval. Then made her way to the pub's somewhat battered old piano, which Oliver and Tom had pushed to the front. Her nose twitched in disapproval as she examined it and tried a few keys.

'It's not a Steinway,' Gennie said apologetically, 'but it is in tune.'

Celia tipped her head to one side, eyes still on the piano's yellowing keys. 'It'll have to do, then,' she said.

Gennie and Oliver had been standing back, watching the rows slowly fill as more and more people arrived. 'I can't believe so many have turned out to support Tom and Caro,' she whispered.

Oliver grunted. His view that curiosity had more to do with the high attendance than religious fervour would be best kept to himself.

A dig in the ribs from Gennie made him look up sharply. 'Look who's here,' she hissed.

'Mum . . . and Will, too. Well, this is a surprise.' He went to meet them.

'I've never missed a Sunday service yet, and this one will be no exception,' Molly said drily.

They were shown to the only vacant two seats in the front row and Gennie

197

wondered if Tom had been reserving them for just this pair.

Molly was resplendent in a pale silk suit and grey pillbox-style hat, which she kept fingering nervously throughout the service.

'Thought I should make a bit of an effort,' she whispered as she passed Gennie to take her seat.

The moving sermon Tom delivered had many of his flock dabbing hankies to their eyes. 'Misguided souls could burn buildings, but they could never destroy the church,' he told them, opening his arms wide to encompass the congregation. 'The church is anywhere its people gather to worship.'

Hymns were sung, intimations read, detailing various local happenings and events. Then Tom thanked Gennie and the Hammonds for the use of the room.

To Gennie's amazement, Molly stood up and made a little speech, saying the family was happy to help, and telling everyone they were welcome at the Flying Fox any time.

Everyone clapped, leaving Molly looking suitably embarrassed.

Tom made his way to the door, ready to exchange a few words of thanks with each member of his flock as they left. Gennie had expected them all to disappear into their cars, or make their way on foot through the village to their homes, but to her amazement, most of the congregation seemed to be turning the other way — in the direction of the bar.

'Looks like we're going to be busy, Gennie,' Celia commented.

Gennie's brow creased into a frown. 'I thought a few more people might stay on for Sunday lunch, but I wasn't expecting as many as this.' She was thankful now that she'd asked Celia's neighbour, Pauline James, who worked as a school dinner lady in the next town, to help prepare Sunday lunches. 'I'd better get through to the kitchen,' she said.

As Gennie hurried off, Molly turned to Will. 'You'd better stay and lend a hand, too, Will. I can drive myself to the hospital.' She glanced towards Will's old Renault. 'All right if I take your car?'

Will scowled at the vehicle. 'I'm not sure it would get you there in one piece. You

199

would be better taking Oliver's Porsche.'

'I can drive you,' Oliver offered — a little reluctantly, Molly thought.

'No need. I can see you want to stay her and help Gennie. I'll drive myself, thank you.' She held out her hand for the car keys.

Oliver pressed his lips together. 'The Porsche can be a bit tricky, Mum. Are you sure you — '

But Molly put up a hand. 'Please don't ask if I'm capable. I've been driving since before you were born.' She gave her son a light-hearted sigh and wiggled her fingers for the keys. 'I promise not to damage your lovely car.'

'It was you I was worried about,' Oliver returned, shooting a glance at Gennie.

She nodded, laughing. Molly Hammond was one of the most capable women she knew. An old Porsche would not defeat her.

With a resigned smile, Oliver handed the keys over, and watched from the kitchen door as his mother manoeuvred her way out of the car park.

Two hours later, Gennie was blowing

her fringe out of her eyes and wiping her damp forehead. 'I can't believe how many Sunday lunches we served today,' she told an exhausted Pauline.

The two women had been so busy dishing up food and serving it that they hadn't had time to tally up the total number of meals. Even Tom and Caro had stayed to eat.

When the bar began to empty, they looked for Gennie in the kitchen. 'I wish I could have given you a bit of warning about that,' Tom said, poking his head round the door. 'But I had no idea so many people would decide to stay for lunch. Maybe you should take bookings next time.'

Gennie waved them into chairs and sank down beside them. Oliver and Will had volunteered to wash up, and were just stacking the final pile of clean plates back into the cupboard. Pauline was pulling on her coat ready to go home.

'You have all been amazing today. I don't know how to thank you,' Gennie said. 'We served forty-five Sunday lunches, not bad considering it's usually about ten.'

Will came forward, drying his hands on a tea towel. 'I've never known the bar so busy, not even on a Sunday lunchtime. You're certainly turning things round here, Gennie.'

'It's an omen,' Caro said. 'A taste of things to come.'

Gennie crossed her fingers. 'I do hope so.'

'I'm off now,' Pauline called, and then stopped, her hand on the back door. 'Does this mean we are opening tomorrow, Gennie?'

'That's not up to me, but I shouldn't think we're likely to be quite so busy on a Monday morning.'

Pauline laughed and gave them all a final wave as the door closed behind her.

'Can anyone smell smoke?' Tom was on his feet, eyes wide with alarm.

Gennie swung round, to check the stove. All the hotplates were turned off and the pots had been washed, dried and put away.

Oliver checked both ovens. 'Nothing overlooked in here,' he said.

'It's coming from outside,' Tom shouted,

202

just as the back door burst open and a panic-stricken Pauline rushed back in.

'Come quickly!' she shrieked. 'The sheds are on fire! The ones attached to the back of the kitchen!'

Oliver sprang into action, pushing Pauline aside as he rushed out, Will and Tom immediately behind him. 'Call the Fire Brigade,' he yelled back. 'The whole building looks set to go up.'

'There are buckets in a cupboard at the back of the function room,' Will shouted. 'I'll get them.'

The smallest of the sheds was not yet alight, but the fire was spreading in that direction, as Will sprinted inside and reappeared seconds later with two plastic buckets and a metal pail.

'The Fire Brigade is on its way,' Gennie called through the smoke as she and Caro filled every receptacle they could lay hands on and began passing them through the open window.

Villagers, hearing the commotion, rushed to help, instructing others to bring more water containers.

By the time the Fire Brigade arrived, a

twenty-strong line of men and women was passing water hand to hand, and somehow managing to keep the blaze in check.

Now and again Gennie caught a glimpse of Oliver, his face blackened by the smoke, working at the top of the line, shouting instructions to the others.

The car park was a black mire of thick smoke and Gennie could hear the volunteers coughing and spluttering as they fought on through it. They didn't stop until the chief fire officer gently moved them aside. 'Let us deal with this now,' he said.

Gennie and Caro had filled a tray with glasses of cold drinks and hugged each volunteer as they staggered into the kitchen. Tom was coughing up black phlegm, and there were angry red burns on his hands.

'Oliver and Will are much worse. You have to get them off to hospital,' he said, gulping for air.

'There's an ambulance on its way,' Caro called, stroking her husband's face.

Gennie tore outside, her eyes frantically

searching for Oliver. It was Will she saw first, and her heart went out to him. His shirt was torn and she could see bare, burned flesh. 'Oh, my God! Are you all right, Will?'

He was bent double, coughing, but he managed to nod, pointing to where the fire was still smouldering in the end shed. 'Check on Oliver. I think he got caught by a falling timber.'

Gennie's heart was hammering as she rushed about, peering into every blackened face to find the one she was searching for. Then she heard her name called and spun round. 'Oliver!' His face was streaked with smoke and blood, and he was holding his arm.

'It's not as bad as it looks.' He tried smiling but it turned into a grimace of pain.

She put her arms gently around him. 'There's an ambulance on its way,' she whispered soothingly. 'Just hang in there, my love.'

She felt his body tense, and he pulled away to stare into her eyes. He looked in so much pain that she had to fight against the tears. Crying now would help no one. She had to be strong.

There was so much mess and commotion around them that she hadn't heard the ambulance's screaming arrival, or noticed the paramedics running towards them. Within seconds they had assessed Oliver's injuries and were leading him to the ambulance.

'Can I go with him?' she pleaded.

But the medic shook his head. 'I think there are more casualties.'

Gennie suddenly remembered Tom and Will. 'This way. I'll take you to them,' she said, picking her way through the snaking fire hoses and burnt timbers.

She and Caro watched as the ambulance, with Oliver, Will and Tom inside and still receiving treatment for their burns, sped away from the Flying Fox.

'It's all right to leave everything here to us now,' the chief fire officer told Gennie. 'If you and your friend want to get off to the hospital.' He gave them a sympathetic smile and nodded around the yard. 'This all looks much worse than it is. I'd say you got off lightly, considering what happened to the church.' He tipped his helmet back from his eyes. 'You might need to replace a couple of sheds, and I've no doubt that the premises will need redecorating, but that seems to be it. The building hasn't been damaged at all, thanks to the speedy actions of everyone involved.'

Gennie was shaking. Right at that moment she didn't much care whether the pub was damaged or not. She kept remembering Oliver's face. She prayed he wasn't seriously hurt.

The forty-minute drive to the hospital in York gave Gennie time to reflect. Had this been another case of arson, as the fire officer had seemed to suggest, or had it been an accident? As far as she knew there was nothing of value kept in the sheds. She remembered a few broken chairs and a couple of tables, plus other pieces of unused bar furniture. She turned to Caro and realised she was trembling. She reached across and squeezed her friend's hand. 'It's fine, Caro. Tom will be fine.'

She could see poor Caro was doing her best not to cry, but her bottom lip was quivering. 'It was like the church all over again. Who is doing this, Gennie?'

'This could just have been an accident.'

Caro shrugged. 'We both know that's not true.'

11

It was the height of visiting time when they arrived at the hospital. With growing agitation, Gennie made two circuits of the car park without finding an empty space. 'I can't believe this,' she complained, smacking her hand against the steering wheel. 'Why is it so busy?'

'Sunday visiting,' Caro muttered, her attention focused on finding that vacant spot. Then she pointed. 'Over there! Look! There's a car just moving out.'

Gennie scanned the row of tightly parked vehicles until she spotted the white reversing lights, then shot smartly forward, indicator light ticking, determined not to lose this space. The departing driver gave her a nod of acknowledgement and she pulled into the spot he had just vacated. Then flopped back in her seat with a sigh.

Caro was already out of the car, calling for Gennie to hurry, and together they ran through the car park and into the hospital reception, following the signs to Accident and Emergency.

It would have been too much to hope the place would be quiet, Gennie thought. Rows of chairs had set out and most of them were occupied by patients waiting to see a doctor.

A nurse at the reception desk looked up when they came in and raised a weary eyebrow.

'We've come to enquire about Tom Dent,' Caro burst out, breathlessly.

'And Oliver and Will Hammond,' Gennie added. 'They were injured in a fire. Can you tell us how they are?'

The nurse glanced at her computer screen. 'Fenwick-cum-Marton?' she enquired.

Gennie and Caro nodded in unison and the nurse smiled. It took all the weariness out of her face.

'They are being attended to at the moment. If you take a seat I'll call you as soon as I have any more information.'

Gennie glanced at Caro's worried face and put an arm around her friend's shoulder. 'Tom will be fine, you'll see,' she said. 'I'm sure the paramedics were just being cautious bringing him here for a check-up.' She bit her lip. The same couldn't be said for Oliver. She remembered the pain on his blood-streaked face, and the burns on his arms, and she winced.

Will hadn't looked so badly injured, but she'd heard stories about young people collapsing after traumatic events like this.

They found a couple of empty chairs against the wall and sat down, their eyes flying to the nurse every time her phone rang. When Gennie eventually accepted that the calls weren't likely to be information about their menfolk, she tried to relax, her glance checking out the others in the room.

She tried to catch the attention of a small boy in the front row with his mother. He whimpered quietly, holding up an injured finger that had been wrapped in what was now a blood-stained handkerchief. Gennie smiled at him, but he buried his head in his mother's chest as she stroked his blond head and soothed him with assurances that the doctor would soon make his finger better.

In another row a young man was cradling an injured arm against his chest, his face contorted with pain. She looked away and glanced at the clock above the reception desk. It was the same as the one above the door into Mitch's ward. Her hand flew to her mouth and she shot out of her chair.

'Molly and Mitch! Nobody's told them.'

Caro stared at her. 'Of course . . . gosh I never thought. There's been so much going on — '

'Molly will be with Mitch now. I have to go up and tell them.'

'Do you want me to come with you?'

Gennie shook her head. 'Best you wait here for any news, Caro.'

As she turned to go, Caro caught her arm. 'Break it to them gently.'

'Of course I will.' The last thing Gennie wanted was to cause Oliver's parents any unnecessary distress.

She was practising the least shocking way of telling them that both their sons were here in the hospital being treated for wounds that they got attempting to stop a fire from destroying the Flying Fox.

She waited for the elevator, chewing her lip. Maybe she would tell only Molly, and let her decide how much Mitch was ready to cope with. But fate took the decision out of her hands for as the lift doors slid open, Molly came rushing out, almost bowling Gennie over.

She gipped her arm, eyes wide, fearing what she might hear. 'What's happened to Oliver and Will?' she demanded. 'The nurse told me they were here, being treated for burns, but she had no details.'

Gennie gently freed herself from Molly's grasp and did her best to smile. 'I'm sure they will both be fine.' She tried to sound confident. 'They are being seen by a doctor now. Tom has also been brought in.'

Molly put a hand to her mouth. 'Tom too . . . ?' Her words died away as she searched Gennie's face for an explanation.

'There was a fire,' Gennie started. 'The Flying Fox could have been burned to the

213

ground if it hadn't been for the three of them. Does Mitch know what's happened?' she asked, as they hurried along the corridor to the A and E department.

Molly shook her head. 'No, thank goodness. The nurse asked me to step out of the ward before she told me.'

Caro jumped to her feet when she saw them push through the double doors. She had found another chair and was guarding it fiercely for Molly. Her face told them there was still no news.

Over the next thirty minutes Molly's expression grew more and more disbelieving as Caro and Gennie described the afternoon's events. Then she sank back into the hard wooden chair.

'And the police think it was arson . . . but why?' She pressed her fingertips against her temples and shook her head. 'I don't understand any of this. It just doesn't make sense.'

'That's how Tom and I felt after what happened to St Stephen's,' Caro said flatly. 'We couldn't find any logic to it either.'

They looked up as the door at the far end of the reception area swung open and

Tom came through. His face was still streaked with soot from the fire as his eyes searched the room for his wife. When he spotted her he threw out his arms and she rushed into them.

'Thank God you're all right,' Caro said, blinking back tears.

'I'm fine, darling, really I am.' He released her and led her gently back to where Molly and Gennie were waiting.

'I feel a complete fraud being here,' he told them. 'But the paramedics insisted on bringing me in the ambulance because I had inhaled some smoke.'

'What about Oliver and Will? They've told us nothing,' Gennie said.

'I think Will is fine . . . a few cuts and bruises. From what I could make out they are going to release him too.'

Out of the corner of her eye she could see Molly visibly relax. At least one of her sons had escaped serious injury. But Gennie's heart was pounding. Her hands had balled into tight fists and she could feel her nails digging into her palms. 'What about Oliver?' she asked, quietly.

Tom's eyes darkened. 'I'm not sure. I

heard the doctors talking about finding him a bed on one of the wards.'

Gennie stared at him. She was remembering holding Oliver before the paramedics arrived and him insisting that his injuries were not as bad as they looked. She could feel tears trembling and turned away. If she gave way to her feelings now it wouldn't help Molly.

Tom understood and touched her arm, but when he spoke it was to Molly. 'Have faith,' he said. 'Both your sons will be just fine. I know they will.'

As though on cue, Will appeared from the same door Tom had just walked through, and Molly hurried towards him. His left wrist was bandaged and he had a plaster over his right eyebrow.

'Just scratches,' he assured his worried mother. 'Poor old Oliver took the worst of it. He pushed me out of the way when one of the wooden beams came crashing down.' He winced and added grimly, 'Both his arms got burned.'

'Oh, no!' Molly cried. 'Don't tell me it's serious.'

'The doctor is coming to speak to us.'

He gave his mother's shoulders an encouraging squeeze. 'Let's wait till then before we jump to any wrong conclusions.'

Gennie fixed her stare on the door. She tried not to imagine the pain Oliver might be suffering. Will had said he had burns to his arms. What else might the doctor tell them?

It was probably no more than five minutes, but it seemed like an eternity before the young Asian doctor appeared, his white coat flying. They all crowded round him, everyone firing questions at the same time. He glanced around the still crowded waiting room, and then nodded ahead. 'I think we'll be more comfortable along here. Please follow me.'

At first Gennie thought they were being taken to see Oliver, but the doctor lead them through a door marked 'Relatives' Room' and her heart sank. Were they about to be told bad news?

But the doctor put his hands up in a gesture that said 'everything's fine'. He said, 'I know you have all been worried, but we are really very pleased with Mr Hammond's condition. He has burns to both forearms, but nothing too serious. He's also cracked a rib.'

Gennie gasped and they all looked at her.

'There are other cuts and bruises,' the doctor continued. 'And he has managed to inhale quite a bit of smoke, but the paramedics gave him oxygen at the scene so we are not expecting there will be any lasting damage to his lungs.'

He paused, looking at each anxious face in turn. 'The good news is that none of his injuries are life-threatening. We will be keeping him in for a day or two for observation, but it shouldn't be too long before he can go home.'

Up in the grey sky the sun suddenly slid from behind a cloud and flooded the small room with light. Gennie wanted to hug herself and dance around the small wooden table with its neat stack of magazines.

'Can I see him?' Molly asked.

'Are you his mother?'

She nodded.

'Of course you can.' The doctor smiled and turned to the others. 'He's also been asking for Gennie.'

Molly looked up sharply and Gennie's face reddened. 'I'm sure he wants to see you first, Molly,' she said quickly.

Molly gave her a questioning smile, but said nothing. If the others thought it interesting that Oliver should be asking for Gennie, none of them showed it. They were too busy sharing their relief that his injuries were not as serious as they could have been.

Gennie's heart was singing. A strange surge of emotion was pulsing through her, making her insides tingle. Oliver would be home in a few days — and he wanted to see her!

For the first time that day Gennie felt herself relax. She didn't mind how long Molly kept her waiting to see Oliver. A mother deserved her time with her son.

When the door to the Relatives' Room opened, they all expected to see Molly return. But the man who walked in was a stranger. At first Gennie thought he must have strayed into the room by mistake, but then she saw the woman behind him.

'It's her!' Caro whispered urgently, giving Gennie a nudge. 'The red sports car woman.'

Gennie swallowed. She'd only ever seen Laura Wells from a distance. Her mind once again raced back to the time she'd seen her kiss Oliver in this very hospital car park. An attractive, middle-aged woman, whose body language suggested she shared an intimate relationship with him.

The Laura Wells who stood before them now looked thin and strained, worry lines etched on her all-too-pale face. The last time Gennie saw the woman, her long blonde hair had been twined into an elegant topknot. Now it hung in untidy strands across her face. She wore a high-necked, long-sleeved dark green sweater and black slacks.

The man came forward, hand outstretched. 'I'm Brian Wells, Oliver's business partner. This is my wife, Laura.'

They all shook hands.

'How did you know Oliver was here?' Gennie asked.

'Molly rang us. She thought we should know. How is Oliver?'

'Someone tried to burn the pub down,' Gennie said flatly. She saw Laura shiver.

'My God!' Brian's eyes were wide with shock. 'She didn't tell us that.' He looked round the room. 'Who would do such a thing?'

'Probably the same person who burned down our church,' Tom said grimly, adding, 'But the police will find the person responsible. I'm sure of that.'

'What about Oliver?' Brian and Laura had both turned to Gennie.

'We've been told his injuries are not as serious as they might have been.'

Laura's hand shook as she felt behind her for a chair, and Brian guided her into it. She looked ready to collapse.

'Is your wife all right?' Tom asked.

'She's been ill. All this has come as a bit of a shock to both of us.' He hesitated. 'Oliver has been a good friend to us.'

Gennie glanced at the figure slumped in the chair. Was Oliver really having an affair with this woman? Right now she looked like the one who ought to be in hospital. She felt a sudden surge of compassion for Laura Wells. She must have got the whole affair idea completely wrong. Oliver had tried to talk to her about Laura. She wished now that she hadn't stopped him.

Molly's face was radiant when she reappeared. She'd obviously satisfied herself that Oliver had suffered no lasting damage. 'He wants to see you now, Gennie.'

As she moved to the door she caught Laura's eye. The woman had looked quickly away, but not before Gennie saw the raw hatred in her eyes. She tried to put that look out of her mind as she walked briskly to Oliver's ward.

He was sitting up in bed, both arms heavily bandaged. He grinned at her look of shock. 'It's not as bad as — '

'I know,' she cut in, laughing. 'Not as bad as it looks. Well, it looks painful to me.' She bent over him and planted a light kiss on his forehead.

He began to open his arms to her, and then winced in pain. 'My cracked rib.' He grimaced. 'I almost forgot. I'm not supposed to move about too much today.'

Gennie stepped back from the bed and tilted her head to give him a critical look. 'I hope you're not going to be a difficult patient.'

He gave her a sheepish grin. 'Wouldn't dream of it.'

She smiled back at him and then her eyes grew serious. 'You gave us all a fright, Oliver. You shouldn't have taken all those chances. That's what the fire service is for.'

'But the Flying Fox is still standing, isn't it?' There was a twinkle in his eye. 'Mum's been telling me the fire was restricted to those sheds.'

Gennie nodded. 'That's right. The fire officer told me any damage to the main building would be minimal. They will have to give the place a proper check over, of course, but I think we got off lightly compared to poor St Stephen's.'

Gennie saw the shadow cross his eyes. 'Mum also told me that it was arson.'

'Hmm . . . it's looking that way. Seems you were right to worry, Oliver. It's just a blessing that this madman chose to strike during the day when we were all up and about.' A shudder shot through her. 'I don't even want the think about what might have happened if the fire had started in the middle of the night.'

'You mustn't even think like that.' He lifted a hand to her and winced with the effort. 'Take my hand, Gennie.'

She rested her fingers in his.

'I said I would keep you safe, and I meant it.'

She looked up, smiling into his eyes, and the connection between them shot through her like a bolt. For a few seconds neither of them spoke, and then Gennie leaned forward and kissed him gently on the mouth. 'Thank you, Oliver,' she said.

She knew now that all the doubts she'd ever had about him were in her imagination. Oliver was not having an affair with Laura. But something was going on.

She took a breath. 'Brian and Laura are here. Molly called them.'

She saw him flinch.

'You don't have to see them. I'll tell them you're tired and want to rest.'

'No,' he sighed. 'I can't put it off forever. Besides, there are practical things Brian and I need to sort out.' He looked up. 'How are they looking?'

'Anxious . . . but in Brian's case I think he is more concerned about his wife than his business partner.'

Oliver raised an eyebrow.

'Laura looks ill, as though she'd just been through a terrible shock.' She hesitated before looking up and meeting his eyes. 'Were you two close?'

Oliver rolled his eyes. 'Hardly,' he said. 'Laura is a sick woman. She's had . . . mental problems. It's worrying about her that has sent Brian almost over the edge.' His fingers picked at the white bedcover. 'She's developed this . . . *fixation* for me.'

Gennie said nothing.

'Lately she's taken to following me. It's unnerving.'

'You mean she's stalking you?' Gennie's voice rose in disbelief.

He nodded. 'Pretty much. I think she's been in my cottage . . . moved things about.'

'That business of Will leaving the back door open?' Gennie pressed her lips together. 'I knew it! I was sure she'd been to your place when she almost ran me off the road that day.' She looked at him. 'You have to do something, Oliver. You can't let things go on like this.'

'I know. It's just a question of what. I obviously can't tell Brian, he's got enough on his plate.'

'But isn't it all part of the same thing? It seems to me that both of them need help, and if you don't take action now . . . well, the problem could get worse.'

'You're right.' Oliver let his head fall back onto the pillow. 'I do need to talk to Brian, but not today. For the moment he just needs to know that I will recover and be back at the office soon.'

Gennie raised a warning finger. 'Don't even think about going back to work yet.'

Oliver's face broke into a teasing grin. 'I can see you are going to be a hard taskmaster.'

'Too right,' Gennie said, laughing back. 'And just so there is no confusion, you will be coming back to the Flying Fox to recuperate when you get out of here.'

'Yes, boss.' Oliver attempted to lift his hand in mock salute, but his damaged rib reminded him that was not a good idea, and he put it down again.

'What about Brian? Do you want to see him now?'

Oliver nodded solemnly. 'You'd better wheel them in.'

When Gennie got back to the relatives' room, Molly and Will were missing.

'They've gone upstairs to see Mitch and tell him what's happened.'

Tom explained. 'They said not to wait for them, that they would make their own way home.'

She nodded, turning to Brian and Laura. 'Oliver would like to see you.'

The woman's eyes widened. 'Both of us?'

'Yes, both of you.'

Gennie, Tom and Caro watched them go.

'There's something not right about that couple,' Tom said.

Gennie sighed. 'You could be right.'

'Well?' Caro was grinning. 'How is Oliver?'

'Much better than I had expected. He's in a lot of pain with the broken rib, but he's in good spirits. He expects to be discharged in a couple of days. I'm insisting he comes back with me to the Flying Fox to recuperate.'

She saw the look that passed between them, and grinned. 'We're just good friends, you know.'

Caro put an arm around her friend's shoulder. 'Of course you are,' she said.

12

The drama of the pub fire was easing by the time Gennie drove Tom and Caro back to Fenwick-cum-Marton. But a few of the locals still gathered in little groups at the house gates. Their body language and glances in the direction of the Flying Fox indicated that the fire was still a hot topic in some circles. Hardly surprising, Gennie thought. Two fires in a week . . .

She'd been about to turn up to the vicarage when Tom stopped her.

'Let's check out the damage at the pub first,' he said.

Gennie shot him a grateful smile. 'I'd been dreading this,' she said quietly, her eyes on the tail end of the fire engine she could see still in the pub car park.

Water from the hoses lay in sooty black pools as the firefighters packed away their equipment. She parked in the road, not wanting to restrict their vehicle's exit. The three of them got out, staring at the charred remains of the outbuildings. The biggest one, where Will normally garaged his car, had been razed to the ground.

Gennie put her hands to her head. 'I still can't believe this. I'm frightened to go indoors and see what the smoke has done to the rest of the building.'

Caro slipped an arm around her shoulders and gave her a squeeze. 'Let's go inside and get this over with,' she said.

Gennie's hand shook as she fumbled with the key.

'It's open,' said a voice from behind her, and she spun round to see the weary face of the fire officer she had spoken with earlier.

'We needed access.' He saw her look of apprehension and added quickly, 'It's OK. The pub is fine inside. Well, there's a bit of smoke damage of course, but nothing serious.' He glanced back at the burnt-out sheds. 'You were lucky.'

Gennie looked past him to where his officers were still clearing away. 'Can I offer you tea?'

'That would be very acceptable.' He

grinned. 'Just a quick brew to wash away the soot.'

'I'll do it,' Caro offered, easing past them to go into the kitchen and fill the kettle. Tom went with her and busied himself sorting out mugs.

Gennie glanced at the blacked wall at the far end of the kitchen where a window had been left open. The fireman followed her gaze.

'There's a bit more of that in the bar, I'm afraid. I'll show you.'

He led the way and she followed, stopping in the bar to stare in dismay at the blackened outer wall.

'Fires are messy things, but this probably looks worse than it really is. A few buckets of soapy water and some elbow grease and you'll get rid of this in no time.'

She gave him a sideways glance. 'I suspect it might take more than just a few buckets.'

'Well, like I said. You've got off lightly. The whole building could have gone up if your friends hadn't acted so quickly. You've got them to thank that the structure of the building is undamaged.'

Gennie's mind went to Oliver, his arms bandaged, his handsome face suddenly contorted with the pain of a cracked rib. She nodded. 'They were all very brave,' she murmured, and then asked, 'Does that mean we could be back in business once this mess is cleaned up?'

The officer nodded. 'I see no reason why not.'

Fifteen minutes later, as the departing firefighters headed for their vehicle and Caro was elbow-deep in suds and tea mugs, Gennie cornered the fire officer on his way out.

'Do you still think this was arson?'

He turned to face her, his grey eyes serious. 'The police will want to talk to you about that, but between you and me, there's no doubt about it.' He paused, as though considering the wisdom of continuing. 'Look, it's not my place to tell you this, but I'm sure you will find out anyway. Small fires had been deliberately set just inside the shed doors, then drenched in petrol.' He sighed. 'Exactly the same as at the church. The arsonist was lucky he didn't go up in flames himself.'

Gennie's eyes widened. 'It was the same person, then?'

The officer nodded. 'Looks very much like it.'

After he'd gone, Gennie turned back into the kitchen to tell Tom and Caro what he'd said.

Tom's brow creased. 'I thought as much,' he said gravely.

'I've just had a horrible thought,' Gennie said. 'You don't think this has happened because we're friends, do you?'

But Tom's hand went up. 'Now stop right there, Gennie. This isn't personal. This arsonist wants to destroy buildings, not people. The church and the Flying Fox are the two most significant buildings in Fenwick. That's why they were targeted.'

But Caro and Gennie were exchanging doubtful looks.

'Stop being so negative you two,' he scolded. 'Let's go have a look at this cleaning job.'

They all trouped into the bar and surveyed the blackened walls.

Gennie screwed up her face. 'This'll take forever.'

'Not if there's enough of us,' Tom said.

Caro clapped her hands, instantly on her husband's wavelength. 'That's a great idea,' she said. 'We can round up the villagers.'

'But not tonight,' Tom said. 'We all need a good night's sleep.' He turned to Gennie. 'Why don't you come back to the vicarage with us? We can easily make up the spare room.' He raised an eyebrow at Caro.

'Tom's right. You can't stay here on your own, Gennie.'

But Gennie shook her head. 'It's very kind of you both, but I can't leave the place unattended, especially now.'

'Well, in that case, I'm staying too,' Caro announced.

'I'd be much happier if you would both just come to the vicarage,' Tom said.

Caro stretched up to plant a kiss on her husband's cheek. 'We'll ring if we have a problem.'

Tom's sigh was relenting. 'What about your night things?'

'I'll come back with you and pack an overnight bag.'

'You really don't have to do this, Caro,' Gennie said, but her protests were waved aside.

After they left, Gennie wandered around the empty building. Caro and Tom were right. Now that she was on her own she realised how much the day's events had shaken her. The last thing she wanted was to spend the night alone at the Flying Fox.

The phone rang in the office, interrupting her thoughts, and she went through to answer it. 'Molly!' Alarm bells were ringing the moment she recognised the voice. 'Has something happened? Is Oliver all right . . . Mitch?

'Everything is just fine.' She could hear the laugh in Molly's voice and relaxed. 'We're worried about you down there on your own. Why don't you come up and stay with us at the bungalow tonight? Will can collect you.'

'Thank you, Molly. That's very thoughtful of you, but Caro's staying with me tonight.'

'Well . . . if you're sure . . . '

'Positive.'

'Actually, Gennie, Will and I would like to have a word with you anyway. Would it be all right if we called down around nine?'

Gennie glanced at the clock and was surprised to see it was already almost seven o'clock. 'That's fine, Molly. I'll look forward to it.'

Gennie replaced the phone then stood staring at it. Now what was Molly up to? And what was so important that she had to see her tonight?

Caro had lost no time in getting back to the pub. Tom was carrying her overnight bag. 'Same room as before?' he asked, already heading for the stairs.

'Yes, thanks Tom,' she called after him.

Caro put the casserole she was carrying into the oven in the kitchen. 'I'm guessing you haven't eaten today?'

Gennie thought back to the bacon rolls Oliver had made that morning and gave a wistful smile. So much had happened since then that it felt like a lifetime ago.

'Now you mention it, I could eat a horse.'

'No horses, just chicken. Will that do?' Caro looked up and gave her friend a rueful grin.

'Sounds perfect,' Gennie beamed back.

Half an hour later the three of them were sitting around the kitchen table eating Caro's delicious casserole with chunks of crusty bread spread with yellow butter.

'That was wonderful,' Gennie murmured, rising to clear away the plates.

'You mentioned Molly was calling in,' Caro said. 'What time did she say?'

'About now, I think,' Gennie said, testing the temperature of the washing-up water in the sink.

'I'll be on my way then,' Tom said, getting up and tilting his wife's chin for a kiss. He touched the end of her nose with his finger. 'You'll ring if there's a problem . . . any problem? Do you hear?'

Caro stood up and clicked her heels, giving him a mock salute.

'Just make sure you do, then,' he repeated, wagging a warning finger at her.

'We'll be fine, Tom. Really we will,' Gennie called after him.

He must have passed Will's car in the car park, for Oliver's mother and brother arrived only seconds later.

Gennie gave them a conducted tour of the fire damage. 'The insurance assessor should be here first thing. We should know more after that.'

Molly shook her head at the blackened walls and sighed.

'I can make myself scarce if you want to talk privately,' Caro offered, when they had all returned to the sitting room.

But Molly flapped her hand, dismissing the idea. 'I think what we have to say might interest you as well.'

Gennie had lit the fire and the room was cosy. At her request, Will poured them all a drink.

Molly sipped her wine and glanced around her. 'It feels strange being back here.' She smiled, nodding towards the old pine dining table. 'That's where the boys did their homework.'

Will gave an exaggerated cough. 'It's where Oliver did his homework. I was usually just messing about.'

Molly pressed her lips together, the

memories flooding back. 'Your brother always was the studious one.' She glanced up at Will with obvious pride in her eyes. 'You were the athletic one.'

'We both played rugby,' he reminded her. 'And Oliver was no mean player if I remember right.'

A sudden image of Oliver, his face smeared with sweat and grime as he kicked a rugby ball high between the goal posts, made Gennie's heart do a strange little flip.

'But we haven't come back to reminisce. It's the future I want to talk about,' Molly said.

They all waited while she took another sip of her wine.

'I talked to Mitch, as I promised, Gennie, and told him about all your ideas for the Flying Fox.'

Gennie blinked. That meeting in the bungalow, when she had talked so enthusiastically about her plans for the place, now seemed like a long time ago. She braced herself, waiting for Molly to break the news gently that they were still putting the pub on the market.

But Molly's face broke into a smile. 'The short answer is yes. Mitch loved your scheme. There are a couple of issues that will need sorting out, and we will have to run your figures past the accountant.' She paused for effect. 'But we are prepared to give you a free hand to run the place along the lines you suggested, but . . . ' She held a finger up. 'If you can't show us at least a sign of improvement in the first six months then we will revert to our original plan to sell the place.'

Gennie opened her mouth to speak, but immediately abandoned that idea. She leapt from her seat and threw her arms around Molly's neck. 'Thank you so much.' She stepped back, embarrassed by her outburst. 'I won't let you down, I promise.'

Caro got to her feet and rushed to hug her friend. 'But this is wonderful,' she enthused. 'If there's anything I can do to help you only have to ask.'

Gennie's head was already buzzing. All the ideas she had put so much effort into compiling were now whizzing through her mind like express trains through a station.

Molly finished her drink and was signalling Will it was time to leave.

'I think the events of the day are beginning to catch up with me,' she said, rising wearily from the comfy old chair.

Gennie touched her arm as she passed. 'I take it this means that Mitch is still on the mend.'

Molly nodded. 'He's making wonderful progress. I think we will have him home in a day or two.'

'How did he take the news about the fire . . . and Oliver?' she asked hesitantly.

'When I left him tonight he was planning to get the nurse to take him down to Oliver's ward in a wheelchair.'

Gennie raised an eyebrow, and Molly sighed.

'I know,' she said. 'But once Mitch sets his mind on something, nothing stops him from getting his own way. He wants you to call in to see him, Gennie, next time you visit Oliver.'

Gennie coloured. 'I meant to do that today, but there was so much else going on — '

'Oh, don't worry. Mitch understands all that. But he would appreciate if you could just drop in on him.' She gave Gennie a knowing look. 'You'll be visiting Oliver tomorrow?'

'I will, and I'll certainly call in on Mitch.'

'Thank you, dear,' Molly said, turning to give Caro a final nod as they left.

'Well, what do you make of that?'

Caro got up. 'I think it calls for another drink. Shall I open that other bottle of wine?'

'Please,' Gennie smiled, holding her empty glass aloft.

Until now she had only given Caro an outline of the plans she had for the Flying Fox. It would be good to talk them out in detail. It would also take her mind off Oliver.

They didn't hear the first knock on the back door, so the caller tried again, more forcefully this time.

Caro looked up. 'Did you hear that?'

They both listened and the knock came again.

Gennie frowned at the clock. 'Maybe Will's forgotten something.'

'I'm coming with you,' Caro said, hurrying after her.

But it wasn't Will.

'Can I help you?' Gennie asked.

The young woman glanced uncertainly from one to the other, her gaze finally resting on Gennie. 'Don't you recognise me, Gennie? It's me . . . Saffi.'

Gennie narrowed her eyes to peer more closely at the girl. Jeans, light grey tee shirt under a short denim jacket, long dark hair plaited with ribbons. Her skin had the velvet bloom of youth and her clear blue eyes were now fixed apprehensively on Gennie's face.

There was no sign of the long flowing Goth clothes, or the exaggerated, theatrical make up.

'It really is you?' Gennie threw her arms wide, laughing.

'Where on earth have you been, Saffi? We've all been so worried about you.'

Saffi was sniffing the air. 'I could smell smoke out there. Have you had a fire?'

'Oh, it's a long story, and it can wait.' Gennie waved the girl into a chair.

Saffi sat down slowly, looking around

her. 'I never thought I would see this place again.' She pressed her hands between her knees, like a child on the naughty step, and raised her huge blue eyes to them. 'I suppose I owe everyone an explanation.'

'You're not a Goth anymore,' Caro observed.

Saffi winced. 'I never really was. I just wore the clothes and did the attitude thing.'

She looked up, catching the amused glance that passed between the other two.

'Oh, I know. I was a pain. I don't think many people round here liked me much. My parents hated the Goth thing too, and blamed Will. But of course, it had nothing to do with him. I just wanted to be as different as I could from those milksops my folks share our farm with.'

'Your parents run a commune, don't they?' Gennie asked, remembering what Oliver had told her when Will returned from his travels.

Saffi's nose wrinkled. 'That's what they call it.' She quoted the commune's motto: '*A place where like-minded souls can find sanctuary.*'

She gave a disgusted sneer. 'The truth is, my parents just want to surround themselves with weak-minded people who allow themselves to be ordered about.'

She saw the look that passed between Gennie and Caro. 'You haven't met them,' she said indignantly. 'They control people, which is why I had to get away.'

Gennie was beginning to get an insight into what made this defensive young woman tick.

'Does Will know you're back?' Caro cut in.

Panic filled Saffi's eyes. 'No . . . and he mustn't . . . not yet!'

'It's all right,' Gennie said, keeping her voice low. 'But poor Will has been frantic. You know he went off to try to find you?'

Saffi nodded. 'My parents told me.'

'The police thought he had harmed you,' Caro interrupted.

'I know. It all got out of hand.' Saffi nodded miserably. 'And it was all my fault.'

Gennie could see she was on the verge of tears, but they were entitled to an explanation.

'Where have you been, Saffi,' she asked gently.

Saffi's chin came up defiantly. 'I went off to have an abortion.'

The two women stared at her.

'An abortion!' Gennie was horrified. 'But why didn't you tell anyone? We could have helped you.'

'If I had you'd have tried to stop me — and the decision had to be mine alone.'

'If you had really made up your mind to do this thing — and I can't say I would have condoned it — then I would have come with you. I would have supported you, Saffi,' Gennie said, shocked. 'You didn't have to go through this on your own.'

'What about Will? Don't you think he deserved to know about the baby?' Caro's voice was a little sharper than she had intended.

Gennie shot her a warning glance. Caro and Tom longed to have children, but so far that hadn't happened. She knew their views on abortion. The last thing this vulnerable young woman needed right now was condemnation. She had trusted her enough to come back. She needed their support.

Saffi was staring down at her hands, fiddling with her rings. 'I couldn't involve Will, not then. I needed to make the decision on my own. I had to do what was right for both me and the baby.' She bit her lip, remembering her desperate plight the night she left.

'So you can see why it's important that Will doesn't know I'm here until I'm ready to face him.'

She looked up at Gennie through long curling lashes glistening with tears. 'Can I stay here?'

Gennie thought of the army of volunteer cleaners Tom was hoping to muster the next day. There was no way she could hide Saffi in a pub full of people who knew her.

'She can stay at the vicarage,' Caro put in quickly.

They both looked up.

'Tom will have to be told, of course, but I'm sure there won't be a problem.'

Gennie gave her an uncertain smile.

'That's kind of you, Caro.'

'It is . . . yes,' Saffi said. 'But I really want to stay here at the Fox. I know the place.' She paused. 'And I feel safe here.'

Gennie shook her head. 'According to Tom, half the village will be arriving here in the morning to help clean up after the fire.'

She saw Saffi's questioning look and explained about the fire, omitting the fact the arson was suspected.

The girl's eyes flew open at the thought of Will having been hurt, but Gennie assured her that his injuries were minor.

'It was Oliver who came off worst.' The mention of his name brought back sweet memories of earlier at the hospital when they'd kissed, and an involuntary smile curved her lips.

She didn't notice Saffi's eyes light up as an idea struck her. 'I could help,' she said excitedly, sitting up, her face animated. 'Well, you two didn't recognise me, did you? I'd be willing to bet that none of the others will either, especially if you introduce me as a friend who is staying over for a few nights.'

She looked from one to the other. 'What do you think?'

'But Will will recognise you,' Caro returned.

'Is Will coming tomorrow? With the best intentions in the world I can't see him wielding a scrubbing brush.'

'You're right,' Gennie laughed. 'I doubt very much if young Mr Hammond will be volunteering his services as a cleaner. Besides, he'll be taking his mother to the hospital.'

'So I can stay?' Saffi's eyes were shining now.

'Yes,' Gennie laughed. 'You can stay.'

13

Saffi was brandishing a spatula as Gennie walked into the kitchen next morning. She was wearing the same clothes as the previous evening, but had obviously showered and brushed her hair into a tidy ponytail. She was liking this new Saffi more and more.

The insurance assessor had called at eight and, after careful inspection of the premises, had confirmed that the Flying Fox was covered for a complete redecoration. He had also agreed to the construction of new outbuildings and told Gennie he had no objection to her friends doing a temporary clean-up to allow the pub to continue trading. So Gennie was also feeling more than a little chirpy.

'Did you sleep well?' she asked.

Saffi frowned. 'I missed Will. It was quite lonely up there without him last night.'

Caro, who had been setting places for

breakfast at the table, cleared her throat and tried not to look disapproving.

'Bacon and eggs all right for you, Saffi?' Gennie asked. 'There's sausage too if you fancy it.'

Saffi put a hand on her stomach. 'I'd rather just have toast and marmalade, if it's OK by you. I'm not used to getting this spoiled.'

'Whatever you want.' Gennie smiled. 'Take a seat.'

The girl was looking decidedly pasty this morning. 'Are you all right, Saffi? You're looking a bit pale.'

'I'm fine,' she assured. 'I suppose it's all just catching up with me.' She glanced out in the direction of the bar. 'What time is everybody arriving?'

'Tom said he would try to get here by nine,' Caro said. She looked up at the clock. He hadn't yet phoned. Did that mean he hadn't been able to round up any helpers? If it were only going to be the four of them, it would take all day to scrub down the walls.

There was a knock on the kitchen door and Gennie went to open it — and then gasped. It looked like half the village, mops, brushes and buckets in hand, had turned out to help. She clapped a hand over her mouth.

'Well, don't just stand there.' Tom grinned. 'Let the workers through.'

Gennie looked back, bewildered, at Caro and Saffi, just in time to see the girl sneak out of the room. Caro came forward and slipped an arm through Gennie's. 'I knew you lot wouldn't let us down.' She grinned around the sea of faces.

'I can't thank all of you enough,' Gennie said.

'Thank us later. We haven't done anything yet,' Celia said briskly, as they all surged into the kitchen. 'I'll organise this, Gennie,' she said. 'You just keep the tea coming.'

'We might need a ladder,' Tom suggested, squinting up at the blackened ceiling.

'We keep a couple of ladders at the back of the function room. I'll check to see if they're still in working order after the fire.'

'I'll do that,' Tom said, taking charge. 'If you and Caro could just show everyone where to fill their buckets and get detergents and stuff.'

Within fifteen minutes everyone had been put to work, Gennie assigning each volunteer to scrub a section of wall. She hadn't noticed Saffi sneaking back into the room, a scarf tied over her dark hair. She'd no idea where she had found the spectacles. They didn't fit very well and kept sliding down her nose, but they certainly did the trick. Even Gennie didn't recognise Saffi.

She noticed some of the others giving the girl curious looks from time to time, and Gennie was quick to tell them that she was a friend who was staying over for a few days — which wasn't altogether untrue. Even Celia seemed to be satisfied with this explanation and stopped sliding inquisitive looks at Saffi.

Tom's little workforce of village volunteers laboured on, with two of the men helping him to scrub the ceiling. By lunchtime the bar looked more presentable. At least they could open until the redecoration work started.

As the others began to tidy away their cleaning things, Caro, Gennie and Saffi disappeared into the kitchen to make a mountain of sandwiches and brew pots of tea and coffee.

'Can you be barman for anyone who wants a drink, Tom?' she asked as he passed through, returning the ladders to the shed.

'Thought you'd never ask.' He grinned.

Molly and Will arrived as the food was being passed around, and at the sight of Will, Saffi took off up the stairs. Caro and Gennie exchanged a look, laughing.

'Have you been to the hospital? How are Oliver and his dad?' Gennie asked anxiously.

Molly pulled out a kitchen chair. 'They're both doing really well. In fact Oliver thinks he might get home later today.'

Gennie's face lit up. 'Really?'

'And Mitch is asking to see you. He wants the full story of the fire and any police update about finding the culprit. Have they arrested anyone yet?'

Gennie shook her head. 'Not as far as I know, but they have promised to keep us informed.'

She poured Molly a cup of tea and offered an egg and cress sandwich before guiding her back to the subject she most wanted to hear about.

'I'll be going over to the hospital later.' It was a huge effort to keep her voice casual. She cleared her throat. 'You think Oliver might get home today?'

'Well that's what he's hoping. Will has offered to collect him, but — '

Gennie didn't let her finish. 'No need for Will to go when I'll be there anyway. If Oliver gets the OK then I can bring him back with me.'

Molly nodded her thanks, satisfied that suitable arrangements were now in place.

Will had wandered through to the bar and was now back with a half-pint of beer in his hand. He lifted an eyebrow. 'There's a frenzy of cleaning going on in there. How did you manage to drum up all that help?'

'We've got Tom to thank for that.' She grinned. 'He turned up this morning like the Pied Piper, with half the village behind him.' She glanced at Molly. 'Just shows how much the locals think of the old Flying Fox.'

*　　*　　*

Gennie knew something was wrong the moment she walked into the ward and saw Oliver's face. Her first thoughts were that he'd been told his injuries were more serious than at first believed. She couldn't bear that. He'd been sitting by his bed, but when he saw her he stood up, arms outstretched. She ran into them.

'What's happened, Oliver?' she asked gently.

He stroked her hair and sighed. 'I may as well tell you. Everyone will know about it soon enough anyway. The fact is . . . I'm ruined.'

Gennie stepped back, staring wide-eyed at him. 'What are you talking about?'

'Brian came to see me yesterday.'

Gennie nodded. 'Yes, I was here when he and his wife came in . . . remember?'

Oliver's face was grim. 'He didn't just

256

drop by to inquire after my health. We've been working on two major contracts. One of them for a new supermarket in Fordham; the other is a leisure centre on the outskirts of York.' He looked up, and she could see the despair in his eyes. He gave a helpless shrug. 'They've pulled out.'

'What! Both of them? But why?' Gennie couldn't keep the shock from her voice.

'Oh, it's simple enough. Word soon gets round when you start letting clients down.' He straightened painfully, wincing as he ran his fingers through his hair. 'Failing to turn up for meetings didn't help, nor did reneging on agreements to supply drawings by an agreed date.

'And then the little mistakes began to creep in . . . a calculation just a fraction out of place . . . figures not interpreted correctly. It all added up.'

Gennie studied him. 'This is about Brian, isn't it? He's the one who's let your clients down. It's hardly your fault, Oliver.'

He sighed. 'But it is. I knew he was

going through a bad time, I thought trusting him with the responsibility of some high-profile work would encourage him to sort himself out. Obviously I was wrong.

'Now it's *my* reputation that's on the line, and just at the moment that isn't worth very much. For a start, I'll have to let the office go. We're already behind with the rent. I don't even have a place to work any more.'

'Can't you work from the cottage? You already have that little office area.'

He shook his head. 'It's far too small. It was only ever intended for basic stuff. I certainty couldn't run an architect's business from there.'

His shoulders suddenly sagged and there was such a look of hopelessness in his eyes that Gennie put her arms around him.

He put a finger under her chin and tilted it up until he could look into her face. 'I'm so glad you're here, Gennie,' he said, his voice cracking. 'You're my rock, you know.'

She swallowed as her eyes filled up. He

used his thumbs to gently stroke away the tears before he kissed her. She wanted the sweet sensation of his mouth on hers to go on forever, but that wouldn't get this problem solved. She stepped back, squaring her shoulders.

'There will be a way out of this, Oliver, and we're going to find it. Now, has the doctor given you the all-clear to leave today?'

He grimaced. 'That's the other thing. They want to keep me another day for tests.'

'Tests?' Gennie's voice rose in alarm.

'I've been having headaches.'

'You never said.'

'They only started this morning. I'm sure it's nothing. I've told them I won't have the tests.'

'Now that would be really silly, Oliver. How do you expect to get your business back on track if your health is under par? You have to stay and let the doctors do what's necessary.'

The trace of a smile twitched at the corners of Oliver's mouth. 'Are you bossing me, Miss Durham?'

Gennie's face broke into a grin. 'Got it in one. Let the doctors carry out their tests. They know what they're doing. If all is well tomorrow then I'll come in to fetch you home.'

He made a resigned grimace. 'OK, I'll stay one day just for you, but I'm definitely moving out of here in the morning.'

Gennie nodded, and traced a finger down his cheek. 'How are the broken ribs?'

'Sore.'

'Poor Oliver,' she said. 'You have been through the wars, haven't you?'

'Not as much as Dad, upstairs. I think he wants to see you, by the way.'

She nodded. 'I'm going to look in on him now. Are you fit enough to come with me?'

'Just try and stop me,' he said, getting up and walking gingerly beside her to the elevator. 'By the way, Dad doesn't know anything about this work business.'

'Don't worry. I wasn't planning to mention it.' The last thing we need is Mitch having another heart attack, she thought.

Mitch Hammond's face lit up when they walked into his room. Gennie went forward to give him a peck on the cheek. 'How's the patient?'

'Here under false pretences. I've just been told I can go home tomorrow.'

'That's great news, Dad. Does Mum know?'

Mitch nodded towards a mobile phone on his bedside cabinet. 'Will brought that in for me. I was just about to ring her, but I think I'll wait for tonight's visiting so I can tell her in person.'

He indicated they should sit, and didn't miss his son's wince of pain as he did so. 'Now Gennie, lass, we have a lot to talk about. Molly's been telling me about all these plans you have for the Fox. Don't look so worried. I heartily approve of all of them. You have our full support to give them a go and see if we can get the old pub back on her feet. She deserves that at least.

'So tell me about the fire. Have you called the insurers?'

Gennie nodded and recounted the assessor's visit. 'He reckons we could have the whole pub redecorated and the outhouses rebuilt.' Her eyes were shining. Why hadn't she immediately thought of that? She glanced up at Oliver. It could make the perfect solution, but she would have to check out the practicalities before she mentioned the idea.

Mitch was looking at his son. 'How are you, Oliver? Any word of you going home?'

Oliver cleared his throat. 'In the morning, hopefully.'

Mitch dropped his head back onto his pillow. To Gennie's mind he still looked pale and tired. 'Tomorrow it is then,' he said wearily. 'And we can all get back to normal.'

They didn't know it then, but 'normal' was the last thing that day would turn out to be.

Gennie walked Oliver back to his side ward, determined to see him settled before she left.

'I'm not going until you get back into bed,' she insisted, concerned at how weak he appeared to be, even after such minor exertion as strolling the few yards to the lift.

He gave her a playful scowl and did as he was told.

She leant forward and kissed his cheek. 'Promise me you will concentrate on getting fit again.'

He caught her hand and kissed the palm, his eyes lingering on her mouth. A delicious shiver raced up her spine.

'Anything you say, Ma'am.' He grinned.

14

Disturbing thoughts were still swirling around Gennie's mind as she drove back to Fenwick. She was positive now that Laura was at the bottom of the knife business. But what did the letter mean? She tried to put this feeling of fear aside and concentrate instead on Oliver's health. He wasn't out of the woods yet; he still had those tests to face. No matter how desperate she was to know the results, she knew his doctor would only discuss his patient's condition with a member of the family.

As soon as she pulled into the Flying Fox car park, she rummaged for her phone and punched in Will's number.

'It's probably nothing, so don't go worrying Molly, but Oliver's been having headaches. His doctor wants him to have some tests.'

'Headaches?' Will's voice was concerned. 'It's probably all those business worries. That partner of his is a nightmare.'

'Oliver told you about that?'

'Not the details, but I know the business is hanging on by a thread. All that nonsense with the police arresting him was the last thing he needed.'

'What exactly did he tell you about Brian Wells?'

'Only that he drinks and has become generally unreliable.' Gennie heard the heavy sigh at the other end of the phone. 'Even I know you can't run a business like that.'

'You're right, Will, but at the moment these tests are the priority. I've no idea exactly what's involved, but he's due to have them in the morning. The thing is, the medics won't tell me anything because I'm not next of kin, but they'll talk to you.'

'I'm taking Mum back to the hospital tonight,' Will said. 'I'll have a word on my own with the doctor and I'll call by the pub later to let you know what he says.'

Gennie was about to thank him when she remembered Saffi. She'd promised not to reveal that the girl was staying at the pub, but it wasn't fair to keep Will in the dark much longer. She'd have to speak to Saffi about that.

'The pub is still closed, Will, so don't bother coming all the way down here tonight, but I would appreciate it if you could ring me.'

Will assured her that he would.

It was after five when Gennie let herself into the pub kitchen. Saffi had been busy and delicious smells were coming from the oven.

'It's fish pie.' She grinned uncertainly. 'I hope you like it. I found some haddock in the freezer. Oh, and Caro's gone back to the vicarage to have supper with Tom. She'll be back around eight.'

Gennie tutted. 'She doesn't have to do that. It's not as if we are in any danger here. I'll ring her now and tell her to stay at home.'

Saffi shrugged. 'I told her the same, but she insisted she'd be coming back.'

She had warmed the plates and was now taking a bubbling cheesy dish from the oven.

Gennie's eyebrows rose in surprise. 'I didn't know you could cook, Saffi. This looks wonderful.'

Saffi beamed at the compliment and again Gennie marvelled at the change in the young woman. 'Will taught me,' she said proudly.

Gennie remembered how many times Will had ushered her out of the kitchen when he prepared one of his experimental dishes. She had to admit he had a knack for producing some very tasty surprises, and if Saffi's cheese pie was anything to go by, she had been a good pupil.

Caro arrived on the dot of eight o'clock, when Gennie and Saffi had settled themselves in front of the TV. The phone rang as she walked in and Gennie got up to answer it.

'Will! Any more news?'

She saw Saffi's head jerk up at the mention of his name.

'Yes,' he said. 'And you can relax because everything is fine. They brought the tests forward. Oliver had a brain scan just after you left the hospital . . . '

He heard Gennie's quick intake of breath and went on quickly, 'The results showed everything was normal. The doctor is putting the headaches down to stress. Oliver can come home tomorrow.'

A wave of relief washed over her. 'That's wonderful news. Thank you so much, Will.'

'There's more,' he said. 'Dad's coming home tomorrow, too. We'll have to celebrate.'

Gennie glanced at Saffi. 'Yes, we will,' she said, smiling.

There was a detective drama on the TV, but no one was watching it. Each of the three women had dramas enough of their own to think about as they sat in companionable silence.

The police search of Oliver's cottage had unsettled Gennie even more than she'd realised. Only people in her immediate circle knew about it so far, but she knew it wouldn't take long for the news to spread, and the whole tragic business of Sophie Chandler's murder would be the main topic of gossip in the village.

Was Oliver mentally strong enough to cope with that? She prayed that he was, but he'd taken so many emotional knocks recently that she wasn't sure.

Saffi announced she was going to bed

when the ten o'clock news came on. When she'd disappeared upstairs, Caro said, 'Has something happened? You've been very quiet tonight.'

Gennie smiled at her friend's intuition. But should she tell her about Oliver's problems? It would be good to share her worries, and she knew Caro wasn't a gossip. As the friends talked, neither of them noticed the hands of the clock creeping on towards midnight.

The back door hadn't yet been locked. They didn't hear the creak as it slowly opened, or the stealthy tread of the intruder's footsteps through the kitchen. Nor were they aware of the knife being slid from its rack by the oven.

They didn't notice her coming into the room and creeping up behind them until it was almost too late.

It was Caro who screamed first, her eyes wide with terror as she stared at the gleaming knife in Laura Wells' hand.

Gennie swung round. 'Laura! What are you doing here?'

The look in the woman's eyes chilled her to the bone.

'Well, isn't this nice,' she purred. 'Both of Oliver's women in the same room at the same time.' Her mouth curved into a chilling smile. 'Hasn't fate been kind to me?'

Gennie could feel her heart thudding in her chest. She had to do something.

'I thought the fires would have been enough to scare the two of you off, but you still went after him,' Laura sneered.

Caro's eyes were wild with fury now. 'It was you?' she screamed at the woman. 'It was you who burned down the church?' She was long past being scared. She was incandescent with rage as she launched herself at Laura. But Gennie's arm shot out to yank Caro back.

The woman was mocking them now. 'I did it for Oliver . . . to make him realise that neither of you was good enough for him.' Then she turned on Caro, her voice full of venom. 'I saw you that night . . . saw that kiss he gave you in the bar.'

Caro frowned, trying to work out what the woman was talking about. And then it dawned on her. 'Oliver kissed my cheek,' she said incredulously. 'He was thanking me for looking after the bar that evening.' She stared disbelievingly at Laura. 'Is that why you destroyed the church . . . because you thought there was something between Oliver and me?'

She made another grab for Laura, but Gennie tightened her grip. 'You burned down the church to . . . to punish me for something I didn't do?' Her voice was rising, and she tried to control it. 'You're mad,' she said coldly. 'You're a mad woman!'

Laura took a swipe with the knife, but Caro stepped back, dodging it.

Laura was jabbing out wildly now, not caring who the blade struck. Then she swung round to Gennie. 'And you,' she screamed accusingly. 'I suppose you'll be denying your relationship with Oliver.'

Gennie's eyes narrowed in disbelief at what she was hearing. 'Why did you set fire to the sheds? Don't you know Oliver could have died?'

Laura bit her lip distractedly. 'Yes . . . that was a mistake. I thought he'd gone. His car wasn't there. I thought he had gone.'

'Oliver's mother took the car to visit her husband in hospital,' Gennie said. 'That's why the car wasn't here . . . but Oliver was. You didn't even bother to check.' Her voice was rising. She took a step forward. 'You could have killed him,' she cried.

'He had to be punished,' Laura said. 'Oliver's been a naughty boy.'

'What are you talking about?' Gennie snapped.

'The other one . . . Sophie.' Laura's eyes were wide . . . staring. 'He brought her here — and she forced herself on my Brian. She had to be punished too, didn't she?'

Gennie stared at her. 'Did you punish Sophie, Laura?' She spoke quietly, fighting to control the growing horror that was now seeping through her.

'She had to be punished,' Laura repeated. 'She was trying to steal my Brian.' Then she smiled, in her own world now. 'I couldn't let her steal my Brian.'

Caro and Gennie stood motionless, staring in horror at Laura.

Gennie moistened her lips. 'What did

you do, Laura?' she asked gently.

The woman's eyes were blazing with excitement. 'I asked her to meet me. We went down by the river. She didn't feel a thing when the knife went in. There was a kind of thud when she fell.' She paused. 'Then she just rolled into the water.'

Gennie was shaking. She heard Caro's sharp intake of breath behind her. 'What about the knife, Laura? What did you do with the knife?'

'I wiped it clean and took it back home, of course.' She smiled. 'Then I gave it to Oliver.'

'It was you who put the knife in Oliver's drawer, wasn't it?'

Laura nodded. 'And the letter as well . . . ' She frowned. 'Brian didn't know I'd found her letter. He'd hidden it under the lining paper of a drawer in our bedroom, you see.

'Sophie shouldn't have written that letter. She tried to split us up, and then she was going to throw Brian away like a piece of rubbish floating down a stream.'

Her eyes glittered with madness. 'He kept her letter. All these years, and he'd

273

kept Sophie's letter. I thought it was time to get rid of it.'

She ran her tongue over her bottom lip to moisten it. 'Oliver's been a naughty boy. He needed to be punished. I hid the letter in his cottage . . . and the knife. Then I phoned the police.'

The woman's cold, calculating admission suddenly filled Gennie with fury and she made a lunge for the knife.

Laura began swiping the blade at her, but suddenly Saffi was there, springing forward and grabbing Laura's arms, pinning them behind her back. The knife flew out of her hand, clattering to the floor.

'Get the knife, Caro,' Gennie shouted, as she helped Saffi to wrestle Laura to the floor.

Suddenly the room was full of noise. Brian had burst in and was screaming at Saffi and Gennie to let his wife go.

Laura called out for him as she collapsed, sobbing. Brian gathered her into his arms, stroking her hair, murmuring soothing words.

'She didn't mean it,' he said, pleadingly, over his wife's head. 'She wasn't really going to harm you. She's ill.'

Gennie caught Caro's look. There was no way they were going to condone Laura's murderous behaviour.

'Your wife burned down the church, Mr Wells, and set the pub buildings on fire. She's admitted as much to us,' Caro said.

'And from what we can gather, she also killed Sophie Chandler,' Gennie said.

Brian Wells nodded, glancing at the knife in Caro's hand. 'Call the police,' he said flatly.

Gennie bit her lip and glanced at Caro, who nodded with a resigned sigh.

Laura Wells was to be pitied.

'Sit here with your wife,' Gennie said, patting the sofa. 'I'll make that call.'

Two young uniformed officers arrived in a police car ten minutes after Gennie's call. She was thankful they hadn't turned up with blue lights flashing and sirens screaming, but she knew some curtains in cottage windows would still have been twitching.

Laura had calmed down, and was weeping quietly in her husband's arms when they walked in. Gennie took them aside and explained the circumstances. The taller of the two PCs jotted the details in his notebook.

'You'll have to come with us now, Mrs Wells,' the other officer said gently.

Laura's face was a picture of confusion as he took her arm, helping her to stand up.

'I'm her husband. I'm coming with you,' Brian said.

'I'm sorry, sir, but you won't be able to do that. We'll look after your wife now.'

'I'm coming anyway,' he insisted, following them out. He hesitated as he reached the door and turned back to look at Gennie, then Caro and Saffi in turn, and there were tears in his eyes when he mouthed 'I'm so sorry'.

'Someone will be back to take your statements, but it will probably wait until the morning,' said the constable, as he put away his notebook.

After they'd gone the three women collapsed into chairs. 'What will happen to her now?' Caro asked. 'I'm beginning to feel sorry for her.'

Saffi raised an eyebrow. 'I can't believe you're saying that. She could have murdered all three of us. And she probably did kill that other poor woman.' She shook her head. 'And she burned down the church and had a good go at doing the same thing to the Flying Fox.'

Gennie sighed. 'It's out of our hands now. Laura needs treatment. At least now she stands a chance of getting it.'

'She needs locking up,' Saffi insisted. 'She could have killed both of you.'

Gennie laughed. 'Not while you were here to protect us.'

Caro leaned forward. 'You were amazing, Saffi. Where did you learn to do a rugby tackle like that?'

The kitchen door burst open and Will come flying in. 'I've just seen the police car. What's happened — '

The words died on his lips as he stared open-mouthed at Saffi. His head began to shake as if he was seeing a ghost.

'Saffi? Oh, my God . . . Saffi!'

He rushed forward, and they were in each other's arms.

Gennie and Caro looked away, smiling.

'I've been nearly out of my mind. I thought I'd never see you again,' he murmured into her hair.

Then he shot Gennie a confused look. 'She was here — and you didn't tell me?'

'Don't blame Gennie or Caro. I asked them to keep quiet about me. I needed to get my head straight before I came to you.'

'I still don't understand,' he said. 'What were the police doing here?'

Saffi led Will to the sofa and sat holding his hand while the three women took turns to describe the evening's dramatic happenings.

His face was a picture of shock. 'Are you sure you're all right?' His gaze flitted over the three of them, but his main concern was for Saffi.

She squeezed his hand. 'We're all fine.'

Will stood up. 'Well in that case I think you have some more explaining to do, young lady.'

Saffi stood up with him and nodded meekly.

'Is it OK with you, Gennie, if I take Saffi back to Oliver's cottage? We have some serious talking to do.'

'And plans to make,' Saffi cut in with a secret smile.

'I think there might be a happy ending coming up there,' Caro giggled after the couple had left.

Gennie nodded. 'I'm sure they will sort everything out. But what about you? Don't you think you should ring Tom and tell him what's happened? You don't want him hearing about tonight from someone else.'

Caro stretched and gave a huge yawn. 'It's the middle of the night, Gennie. If I ring him now he'll panic and come flying over here. All I want now is to slip into a warm bed and sleep for hours. I'll ring Tom first thing in the morning.'

Caro called Tom as soon as she woke up next morning, and he'd come rushing over to the pub just as she had predicted. His face registered all shades of shock and confusion as his wife told him that Laura Wells had burned down the church.

'Poor demented woman,' he said sadly.

'You're very forgiving,' Caro said, putting her arms around her husband.

'But you're right. Nothing can bring St Stephen's back.'

'Not as it was, certainly,' Tom agreed. 'But maybe . . . '

He didn't finish the sentence and Caro and Gennie stared at him.

'I may have some news on that front later today. Let's just say I'm doing a lot of praying.'

Gennie set off for the hospital shortly after nine. She could hardly wait to see Oliver again. The thought that in an hour's time she would be driving them both back to the Flying Fox sent a shiver of excitement though her. She had so much to tell him that she wouldn't know where to start.

He was waiting for her as she walked into the little side ward. 'Let's go,' he said, winking at one of the nurses. 'Before they change their minds.'

'You're in better tune today,' Gennie laughed, as they made their way down to the hospital car park.

'Beautiful ladies always cheer me up,' he said, giving Gennie a lingering smile.

'Well, that's good, because I have an

idea that might improve your mood even further.'

He arched an eyebrow at her.

'You'll have to be patient until we get back to the pub. It will all make more sense when we get there.'

'I'm intrigued,' Oliver said.

'I hope you'll be happy too when you hear my suggestion.'

On the drive back to Fenwick she told him about Laura. For a second he looked stunned. 'She killed Sophie?' he repeated. 'Oh, my God! Did Brian know?'

'I'm not sure.' Gennie winced. 'But I suspect he did.'

For the next few miles Oliver stared ahead in stunned silence. Gennie wished she hadn't blurted out the whole story like that. He was bound to be shocked. Then he said, 'It was Laura who burned down the church?' He shook his head. 'I'm sorry, Gennie. I'm struggling to take all this in.'

'She also started the fire at the pub . . . the one that landed you in hospital.'

'But why? Why would she do such terrible things?'

Gennie moistened her lips before speaking. 'Laura killed Sophie because she believed Brian was falling for her. They probably had an affair . . . I don't know.

'The fires were all about you, Oliver. She was in love with you. In her sick mind she believed that Caro and I were trying to take you away from her. She set fire to the places we loved best as a kind of punishment.'

Oliver was still shaking his head in disbelief as they drove into Fenwick-cum-Marton. 'Poor Brian. No wonder he's as messed up as he is. He's totally devoted to that woman.'

Gennie sighed. 'Well, let's hope they both get the help they need now.'

'You've been having an eventful time since I last saw you. Any more surprises up your sleeve?'

'As a matter of fact, I have.' She looked at him and grinned. 'Saffi's back. She and Will are over at your cottage.'

Oliver's mouth fell open. He was remembering the terrible time the girl had put his brother through. 'Where on earth has she been?' he asked angrily.

'It's a long story, but they are both fine. Don't be too hard on her. I think you'll find that Saffi has grown up quite a lot since you last saw her.'

'I just hope Will knows what he's doing if he takes her back,' he said, going into the pub's sitting room and carefully lowering himself onto the sofa.

He sighed as he sank back. 'You can't imagine how good it is to be here. This place is a little oasis of calm in the storm that is my life at the moment.'

He reached out for Gennie's hand and pulled her down beside him. 'I've been dreaming about this,' he said, as he took her face in his hands and brushed kisses all over it.

Gennie's heart was singing; the sensation of his kisses was too exquisite for words.

'Tell me I'm not getting the wrong messages, Gennie,' he whispered, nuzzling her neck. 'Because I'm falling in love with you.'

Gennie nestled closer. 'You don't know how long I've waited to hear you say that. I love you, too, Oliver.'

He suddenly pulled back. 'What am I

doing? I have no right to say these things to you. I don't even have a business any more.'

Gennie studied his worried face. 'Surely things aren't that bad?'

Oliver pursed his lips, thinking. 'I have a couple of small contracts that will just about keep things ticking over, but apart from that . . .'

'But that's all you need, Oliver. You can build on that. I'll help you.'

As he was about to pull her closer again there was a knock on the kitchen door.

'What now?' Gennie muttered, getting up to answer it.

'Oh, Tom, it's you. I was afraid it might be the police come back to ask more questions. Come through.' She led the way back into the sitting room. 'Oliver's here.'

'I was rather hoping to find you two together,' he said.

He had a look in his eye that Gennie couldn't quite fathom. 'Is Caro all right?'

'Caro's wonderful. We've just had some good news, actually.' He rubbed his hands together. 'I've just heard from the Bishop.

He's been given the go-ahead to build our new church.' He grinned delightedly. 'So St Stephen's will live again.'

Gennie threw her arms around his neck. 'That's wonderful, Tom. I can't tell you how happy I am for you and Caro.'

Oliver got up with difficulty and extended his hand. 'That's brilliant news, Tom. Congratulations.'

'There's more,' Tom said, his eyes on Oliver. 'How would you feel about designing our new church?'

They both stared at him. 'Are you serious?' Oliver said.

Tom nodded. 'Never more. The church works with architects who specialise in religious buildings, but none of them would treat the project as sensitively as I know you would. Your family has been connected to St Stephen's for generations. I know how much the old building meant to you.'

He went on, 'We will obviously have to seek quotes from some of your colleagues, but I know the quality of your work, Oliver, and my opinion will have a lot of sway.'

It was all Gennie could do to stop herself from jumping up and down and dancing round the room.

But Oliver was hesitating. 'I'm hugely flattered, Tom, but this would be a massive undertaking and my business has been having a few problems recently. To be honest, I don't even have an office any more.'

Tom nodded. Caro had put him in the picture about the damage Oliver's partner had done to the business.

'But that's the other thing I had to tell you, Oliver,' Gennie cut in excitedly.

Oliver gave her a quizzical look.

'The outbuildings,' she said. 'The pub is insured to have them rebuilt. You could have the large one for your new office.'

Oliver's frown slowly melted into a delighted grin. His eyes lit up. 'But that's genius!' He threw his arms around Gennie, and then winced as he was reminded about his damaged ribs.

'I don't expect it would take very long to get them rebuilt. You could be working from there in no time. And there's plenty of space around here to set up your drawing board in the meantime.'

'It sounds to me like the problem's been solved,' Tom said. 'Can I take it that the new St Stephen's has its architect?'

Oliver shook Tom's hand even more vigorously this time. 'Vicar . . . you have a deal!'

15

'Mitch is home!' Molly announced when Gennie picked up the phone. 'Can you and Oliver come up to the bungalow this evening? We're planning a champagne celebration.'

Gennie glanced across at Oliver. 'We'd be delighted,' she said happily.

'I don't suppose you've any idea where Will is? He took me to the hospital to collect his father, but we haven't seen him since. And his mobile is switched off.'

Will had obviously not told his parents about Saffi's return.

'I'll try to track him down for you.'

'Thanks, Gennie. We want all the family there tonight.'

Gennie put down the phone and frowned. Maybe Will had taken off again after Saffi told him about the abortion. Just when things were going so well for everybody, too.

The bar had temporarily re-opened,

and Celia was back in her domain serving drinks to thirsty locals when Will and Saffi tapped on the sitting room door and walked in.

Oliver and Gennie looked up in surprise.

'You'd better sit down,' Will said. 'Saffi has something to tell you.'

Oliver was staring at Saffi. He couldn't believe the transformation. 'Whatever you've done to yourself, I definitely approve. I almost didn't recognise you, Saffi.'

Gennie gave him a nudge. 'I told you how much she'd changed.'

A shy smile was beginning to play around Saffi's mouth. 'I didn't tell you everything, Gennie . . . about the abortion, I mean.'

Oliver's eyebrows went up. 'Abortion? You've had an abortion?'

'Let her finish, Oliver,' Will cut in.

Saffi took a deep breath. 'It was true that I went off to get rid of the baby. I thought at the time that it was what I wanted. I just couldn't see myself looking after a baby. But it was a serious decision and I felt that I had to make it myself.' She reached out and took Will's hand. 'I know now how wrong I was. I should have told Will about the baby. We should have made the decision together.'

'What did you mean, you didn't tell me the whole truth?' Gennie asked quietly.

'I didn't have the abortion.' She laid a hand tenderly on her stomach. 'I'm still pregnant.'

Gennie was off the sofa in a split second, hugging both of them. 'Oh, Saffi. That's wonderful news. I'm so happy for you both.'

'So I'm going to be an uncle?' Oliver struggled to his feet, grinning, shook Will's hand, and then decided a hug would be more in order.

'I'll need to find myself a job and somewhere to stay, but the important thing is that we are back together again,' Will said, his arm around Saffi.

'I can maybe help you out with accommodation,' Oliver said, looking at Gennie. 'I've been invited to stay at the pub for the next week or two. You can have the cottage.'

Gennie came forward and slipped her arm through Oliver's. 'Of course, if you stayed here on a more permanent basis, Saffi and Will could rent the cottage from you.'

'Suits me.' Oliver smiled, gazing into Gennie's eyes.

'Really? But that's great,' Will said. 'Although I'd have to find myself a job before I could afford to pay you rent.'

'How do you fancy being our contract chef?' Gennie asked.

Will shrugged. 'But I'm not a chef.'

'Not officially, perhaps, but I've tasted your food, and it's great.'

'What's a contract chef?' Saffi asked.

'Someone who's not actually on the payroll, but who provides a service and takes the profits,' Gennie explained. 'You remember, Will? I mentioned it at that meeting we had the other week.'

Will nodded. 'So I would plan the menus, supply the ingredients and cook the dishes?'

'That's right. You would also be responsible for employing any kitchen and waiting staff. But after that, all the profits belong to you,' Gennie explained. 'It's kind of like running your own business within a business. I've known it to work very well in other places.'

'Oh, I don't know. You have a lot of faith in my ability to cook.'

'You will be a brilliant chef,' Saffi said. 'I'll help you. What do we have to lose?'

'So we have a deal?' Gennie asked, extending her hand.

Will shook it, laughing. 'Why not.'

★   ★   ★

'Are you sure Will's coming?' Molly asked, frowning at the clock on the mantelpiece.

'Stop fretting. We said to be here for eight, and it's only five past,' Mitch said.

'Oh, he'll be here all right.' Oliver beamed at his parents. 'He has something very important to tell you.' He took Gennie's hand. 'We both have.'

Molly put down her glass of sherry. 'What did I tell you, Mitch? I knew there was something going on between you two.' She came forward, arms outstretched to gather them both into a hug.

Mitch stood up and eyed them expectantly. 'What exactly are we celebrating?

'Gennie has agreed to become my wife,' Oliver said, his eyes full of pride.

'Well, good for you, son. You've landed yourself a bonnie lass.' He also hugged each in turn. 'And our Gennie, here, has got brains into the bargain.'

Gennie blushed and was glad that Will and Saffi had chosen that moment to arrive.

Molly and Mitch both stared at the girl. Will threw his head back and laughed. 'It's Saffi. Don't you recognise her?'

His parents exchanged a look.

Saffi stepped forward. 'I know I didn't exactly make a lot of friends in this village before, but I've changed. Will and I love each other and I really will try harder, if you'll give me the chance.'

She reached into her bag and pulled out a dog-eared bundle of £50 notes. She swallowed hard, and Gennie saw Will's arm tighten encouragingly around Saffi's shoulders. 'It's all there . . . five thousand pounds. I only borrowed it,' she said, giving Mitch a sheepish look. 'I know I should have asked first, and I'm sorry. I would have paid it all back, but it turned out that I didn't need it in the first place.'

She glanced up at Will, and he nodded. Saffi cleared her throat. 'And you're going to be grandparents because Will and I are having a baby.'

For a second nobody spoke, and Gennie swallowed a lump in her throat. Then she saw a tear glistening in Molly's eye as a slow smile spread across her face. 'Come here, Saffi.' She held out her arms. 'Welcome home.'

Over the next half hour the champagne corks popped as Will told them about his new position as chef at the soon-to-be revamped Flying Fox. Molly and Mitch nodded their approval of Gennie's idea to convert one of the new outhouse buildings into an office for Oliver's business.

Everybody's eyes widened when he revealed that he'd been invited to design Fenwick-cum-Marton's new St Stephen's Church.

Mitch sank back in his chair and looked around the happy faces of his family. 'Molly and I are so proud of all of you.'

Molly looked away, wiping at a tear.

'When will the new church be built?' he asked.

Oliver took Gennie's hand and smiled across at Oliver and Saffi.

'Not long, hopefully. Tom's already got a couple of weddings booked.'

'Of course we'll need to find a great venue for the receptions,' Mitch laughed.

'I think I might know a place,' Gennie said with a twinkle.

THE END

We do hope that you have enjoyed reading this large print book.

Did you know that all of our titles are available for purchase?

We publish a wide range of high quality large print books including:
Romances, Mysteries, Classics
General Fiction
Non Fiction and Westerns

Special interest titles available in large print are:
The Little Oxford Dictionary
Music Book, Song Book
Hymn Book, Service Book

Also available from us courtesy of Oxford University Press:
Young Readers' Dictionary
(large print edition)
Young Readers' Thesaurus
(large print edition)

For further information or a free brochure, please contact us at:
Ulverscroft Large Print Books Ltd.,
The Green, Bradgate Road, Anstey,
Leicester, LE7 7FU, England.
Tel: (00 44) **0116 236 4325**
Fax: (00 44) **0116 234 0205**

WREATH FOR A LADY

John Glasby

When Mike Torlin takes on the job of investigating the strange happenings at Pete Donati's carnival ground, he figures it's a straightforward case of somebody wanting to put Donati out of business. Then a peculiar chicken is produced out of an egg: a dead girl, shot with slugs from her own shooting gallery. No killer can sidetrack Mike Torlin for long and get away with it — and when the final showdown comes, he is forced to stand his ground and face up to the killer . . .

MORTAL PROSE

Geraldine Ryan

When a mogul of the literary world is murdered, D.I. Casey Clunes is on the case — though the victim's unpopularity ensures no shortage of suspects . . . Isobel is an intelligent woman . . . except when it comes to her new toyboy. Still, their relationship couldn't harm anyone else — or could it . . . ? The audience gasps as the new portrait of the headmaster of St Martin's is publicly revealed — defaced — followed by news that the headmaster himself has been shot dead by an unknown assailant . . . Three stories of mystery and murder from the pen of Geraldine Ryan.